CW01091519

THERE SOMETHING
YOU SHOULD KNOW

BY WENDY TEW

CHAPTER ONE

Alison Jones always thought, on meeting someone for the first time, that they would like her. It was not that she was vain, far from it, but she invariably took this optimistic view. It surprised her then, when she was introduced to a woman at a party, to see in the other's eyes a reserve, hostility even. She shrugged it off, turned away to meet kinder faces but, looking back, Alison remembered that moment as the start of it all.

The party was being held in a detached house at the end of an avenue of similar houses in the village of Westwood where Alison and Jack lived. Their cottage was in the centre of the village, in the old part, but they could easily walk home from the party and so avoid the undignified tussle, carried on in what they thought were hushed tones in numerous bottle strewn kitchens over the years.

"No, I drove to the Wilson's last Friday, remember?"

"Yes, but we agreed that, as these are your friends and I don't really like anyone here, I could drink tonight."

The latter comment usually being spoken rather louder than intended.

Friends from London were puzzled at such discussions and would say: "Oh, let's just get a cab, we'll pay," not realising that one had to book the only taxi weeks in advance and even then would have to endure the driver's wife's sarcasm.

"A taxi for next Saturday you say. There AND back. Are you quite sure you don't want Mr Clarkson to wait outside while you eat your meal? He'll have nothing better to do."

Walking into the party, Alison found her friend Carolyn, whose birthday they were celebrating, standing in the kitchen clutching a glass of Champagne.

"Caro! Happy birthday. You look lovely. You know I've always loved that dress. Every time you wear it, it just looks better and better."

1

"And I adore your dress too, Ali. At least I did until last week when I gave it to the local charity shop."

Each time they met they invariably exchanged mock insults with each other. They had been friends for years, since their children were small and, having supported each other through various catastrophes of normal family life, they had the easy familiarity of sisters.

"Quick, have some of this Champagne before I drink it all. Now, tell me honestly, how old do I look tonight? Seventy-nine? Ninety-four?"

Ali laughed and, accepting a glass said, "You look about twelve. I wish I did. Last week I saw this middle-aged woman with bad posture and awful hair and realised it was me reflected in a shop window."

The friends went to find another bottle and the party continued in the way parties do when the guests and the surroundings are familiar. Voices grew louder; those who invariably drank too much, drank too much; those who always danced, danced and those who stood around in the kitchen getting in everyone's way, got in everyone's way.

Later, when someone had put on a slow, sultry CD, Ali looked around for Jack, realising that she hadn't seen him for some time. Suddenly, he was beside her and they danced closely together for a few beats before he pulled away and said, "Let's go and get a last drink before we head off." Ali was surprised because her husband was one of those rare men who liked to dance and did it well. As she followed him into the kitchen she saw that the unfriendly woman was standing in the hall and she had a feeling that the woman had been watching her: her and Jack.

Having gone to bed feeling strangely uneasy, Ali was pleased to find that her mood was bright and sunny as she drove to her office the next morning. The weather too was crisp and clear and she swung her little Honda around the country lanes, singing along loudly and tunelessly with the radio. She was a solicitor, had gone into the law a little later than most and had been relieved and delighted to discover that she found her work interesting and rewarding.

Cassell Brookes and Little had their offices in a lovely Georgian building in Barton Casey, a market town not far from Westwood. Ali sometimes wished that she worked in the city in an enormous glass tower and was greeted each morning by an Armani clad receptionist. Instead, there was June, plumply friendly, whose typical comment would be: "Your nine o'clock's already here; nice shiny shoes – he's sure to pay his bills on time."

However, she'd qualified when her daughter Lucy was quite small and it was convenient to work near to home; besides, she'd promised herself at Law School that she'd work for a firm with three names.

Ali remembered her first week with amusement. The senior partner, Mr Brookes (Mr Cassell, if he ever existed, was not in evidence) called her into his office and, throwing his car keys across his desk, told her to move his Jaguar which he'd double parked outside. She realised now, of course, that it was a test and she should have refused or, at least, picked up the keys and quipped gaily, "I didn't realise it was that kind of firm." However, she moved the damn car and ignored an impulse to scrape the wheels against the kerb.

His next test, on her fourth day at work, was to tell her to represent a client in the local Court in a dispute over an unpaid bill. Ali read the papers at least twenty times, wrote down word for word everything she should say, presented her case and won; the Registrar found in her favour. Clearly she was a born advocate and her feeling of euphoria lasted until, getting up to leave the Court, she heard the Registrar say, "No doubt you will be making an application for costs, Mrs Jones?"

Oh God, costs; no one in the office had mentioned costs.

"Err, yes, Sir, of course. I hereby on behalf of my client

and, um, with the Court's permission hereby make an application for costs. Please. Thank You. I rest my case."

The latter words were accompanied by a sort of bobbing curtsey, the kind a small child may give to a minor visiting royal.

The Registrar, whom Ali later got to know well, hid his smile and granted her request.

Things improved quite quickly after that, although there remained moments of embarrassment. Once, when trying to reach a reference book on the top shelf of the firm's library, she'd trodden on a lower shelf, which promptly broke into two pieces, spilling volumes 22-30 of Halsbury's Statutes onto the floor. Gingerly notifying the firm's rather strict female librarian of her dreadful deed, Ali said, "Oh well, I suppose this means I'll now have to sleep with Harold."

And both she and the librarian broke into laughter at the thought of the firm's handyman (short, squat and slightly smelly) going like the clappers on top of Land Law and Practice.

A few days after the birthday party Ali let herself into the cottage she shared with Jack and, after pouring herself a glass of wine, wandered from room to room noting with pleasure that her cleaner had been and the house smelled deliciously of polish and lemons.

Originally three tiny cottages, now knocked into one, French doors had been installed in the rear kitchen, study and sitting room so that light flooded in from the pretty courtyard garden. When Ali and Jack had first moved to Westwood the only house they'd been able to afford had been a rather soulless 1970's semi, built of pale brick and so their current home with its pale grey kitchen and handsome square sitting room was a constant delight.

Jack travelled a lot with his work, often staying away overnight and their daughter Lucy was away at university so Ali was alone in the cottage. She didn't resent this; both of them said that time apart was good for their marriage.

Quite often they wouldn't speak on the phone until he returned, even if he was away for three or four days. Ali was quite scathing about colleagues who would call their partners several times a day. Only last week she'd said to Jack, "Honestly, David at work, his wife called his mobile three times during our Wednesday marketing meeting. Something about Lemongrass – pathetic."

And so, Jack knew better than to call.

Ali switched on her laptop and saw with pleasure that Carolyn had emailed her some photos of the party. She scanned them quickly, looking only at the ones of herself. Once satisfied there were none which showed her with a double chin or mad hair (good old Caro must have edited them), Ali went back and looked at each photo more carefully. There was one of that unfriendly woman, some nice ones of Jack and then some more of the woman (blimey, Carolyn must have a bit of a girl crush; she'd have to speak to her about that) and then finally, there were three photos which Ali stared at for a long time before closing her laptop and going up to bed.

At 2am, she gave up trying to sleep and found Carolyn's email on her phone. Scrolling down to the last three photos, Ali examined each in turn. The first showed Jack and the woman in conversation. He was clearly telling a story, his hands thrown characteristically wide whilst she was grinning broadly. In the second, taken in the hallway, the woman was looking down, a small smile on her lips and Jack was leaning towards her with his hand on the wall beside her head. The final photo showed the woman in the process of leaving the house. She was framed in the doorway, looking back over her shoulder into the hall. A man's arm was just visible around her waist, holding it tightly. Jack's watch, Jack's arm.

The next morning Ali shut herself in the boardroom at work and called Carolyn. As she told her friend of the photos, the conclusions she had drawn in the early hours sounded a little ridiculous. The formality of her surroundings compounded this view; the heavy mahogany furniture and portraits of stern faced judges were not conducive to outbursts of emotion and had calmed many a hysterical divorcee or potential bankrupt over the years. Ali found herself readily agreeing with her friend's opinion that she was overreacting.

"I mean, Ali, women always fancy Jack. I'd sleep with him myself if I could find a bra which matched my pants. You're being silly; you know he absolutely adores you, crazy as that may seem."

It was true. Jack had always been handsome but somehow he'd got better looking as he reached his forties. She'd got used to other women giving him the eye. When they'd look up at him from under their eyelashes she and Jack would laugh about it later. Jack always said that their coy looks reminded him of Princess Diana. But he always made Ali feel special and it was rare for her to be jealous or insecure, as she was that day.

"Who is she anyway?" Ali asked. "I haven't seen her around before."

"No, they're new to the village; Sarah and Chris Hill. They bought one of those five-bed executive places on the old factory site. I met her at the gym. I think you'd like her, Ali. She's quite a good laugh."

Carolyn paused: "Erm, actually I was going to call you anyway. I've invited the Hills over on Friday and I was hoping that you and Jack would come too. Obviously, if you'd rather not…"

Ali was feeling foolish and wished that she'd never mentioned the photos to Carolyn.

"Yes, of course we'll come. That would be lovely. About eight? I'll bring my Pavlova."

Putting the phone down, Ali felt a lot better and, giving a cheeky grin to Lord Denning, whose portrait took pride of place on the boardroom wall (now he would never have made a fuss over some silly pictures), she walked briskly back to her office.

CHAPTER TWO

Sarah Hill never thought that she would be the sort of woman to have an affair and certainly not with someone else's husband, but it had just happened. She knew it was wrong, of course she did, but it was just so exciting. She craved Jack's voice on the phone, the smell of his aftershave. It was though she was addicted to him; nothing seemed as important as arranging their next meeting.

The first time she'd seen him was when she'd gone to pick up her husband Chris from the golf club. She'd been early, the men were still on the course and so, when she'd at last managed to attract the barmaid's attention, she ordered a gin and tonic whilst she waited.

From her bar stool she could see into the club's dining room where a couple in late Middle Age were having an early lunch. Both had dressed up for the occasion; the man, who had startlingly black hair brushed straight back from his forehead, wore a jacket and tie whilst his wife, whose equally raven hair fell in lacquered ringlets down her back, was encased in lilac chiffon.

Neither spoke a word as they chewed determinedly, accompanied only by the sound of their cutlery, wielded like pencils in their resentful fists.

Sarah wondered why they hadn't prepared some topics of conversation before they went out; she sometimes did before an evening with Chris. But then she realised that it wasn't that they had nothing to say to one another, they no longer had any desire to hear the other's reply. They were utterly disinterested in each other.

She turned away from the couple to see her husband Chris and another man walking towards her. Blonde and petit herself, Sarah was usually attracted to dark, wiry men, like her husband, who was often mistaken for a local when they travelled in Southern Europe. The man with Chris was tall and powerfully built with fair hair lightly touched with grey. As he raised his drink, she noticed the blonde hairs on his forearms and felt a wild compulsion to touch them.

Suddenly, Sarah realised that the conversation had stopped and both men were looking at her. Oh God, surely she hadn't actually stroked his arm? No, both hands lay chastely by her side and she pushed them into the pockets of her jacket in case they rebelled.

"Sarah, you were miles away," Chris said. "Jack was just asking if you played too."

"What? Oh yes, golf. I do actually, a little. I'm not very good yet."

Jack smiled at her. "In that case you'll have to give me a game. I always prefer it when I win."

Oh no, thought Sarah, blonde and arrogant; so not my type, not my type at all. But he was of course.

Normally, Sarah would make a joke about meeting an attractive man, but when Chris laughingly said that he'd have to have a drink with Jack every week as it was the first time he'd seen the rather sullen barmaid smile, she changed the subject. Later she wondered why and realised that she didn't want to discuss her first meeting with Jack with anyone; she wanted to keep it all to herself.

Sarah had known Jack for five weeks and been sleeping with him for four when she met his wife for the first time. Jack never talked about her much but she'd definitely got the impression (from him surely) that Alison was rather plain; had let herself go, as her mother would have said. The vivacious redhead who strode so confidently into the party at Carolyn and Trevor Markham's house and proceeded to circle the room, waves of laughter following in her wake, was not at all what Sarah had expected. She couldn't stop herself from staring at her; the full figure carried off by her height, the wide mouth and green eyes, which were slightly slanted at the sides, like a cat.

By the time she'd managed to get a word with Jack, Sarah had had just about enough of the Alison Jones show and just about enough gin to make her feelings clear. But

Jack first made her laugh and later he told her that he'd go mad if he couldn't kiss her and so, when they managed to slip outside unnoticed, she didn't say a word but just allowed herself to enjoy Jack's murmured endearments. Besides, she knew he was married and it was her and not Alison who Jack found "so gorgeous, just bloody gorgeous" that night.

Ali walked along the High Street in Barton Casey on Friday lunchtime. She wanted to buy some cream to add to the Pavlova she had made the night before. Passing the bakers, she grinned to herself and went in. The shop made and sold excellent bread but they also displayed astonishingly primitive fruit tarts, topped with lattice pastry so thick and uneven they looked exactly like something her daughter Lucy used to make from playdough when she was small. Pointing to the most crudely made tart on display, Ali paid the surprised shopkeeper and grinned once more. She'd proudly present the awful tart as her contribution to tonight's dinner party, before casually saying: "Oh, and I made this Pavlova too." Carolyn would catch on straight away of course, *but let's see if Sarah Hill really does have a sense of humour*.

Before returning to her office, on impulse Ali went into LBD, a ruinously expensive dress shop owned and run by the very chic wife of a client. Suzie, the owner, was not there and the bored looking assistant seemed quite happy to let her browse. Suzie tended to pounce if you looked at any item for longer than five seconds. Carolyn and Ali called it "the five-second rule", and would say, "Quick, avert your gaze now or it will be in a statement carrier bag before you know it."

Ali's eye was caught by a silk dress of pale turquoise, very plain with three quarter length sleeves. Trying to avoid looking at the price tag, Ali gestured to the assistant that she wanted to try it on.

One of the reasons that LBD was so popular was because of its changing room. It was much larger than average, softly lit and dressed as though it were a bedroom in a French Chateau. There was even a bed, piled with cushions, onto which you could flop in despair if the clothes failed to live up to expectation (in other words, didn't fit). This time, however, the dress looked lovely and, even better, it was a size 12. A 12! In M&S Ali was a 14 long and, on one unhappy trip to River Island with Lucy, she'd struggled in the minute changing cubicle to fit into a size 16. She'd wear it tonight and not even the horrendous price dimmed her happy mood as she swung the black and pink carrier bag down the High Street.

Getting ready for bed, Sarah congratulated herself. She'd hardly even glanced at Jack all evening; instead, she had chatted to the two women and flirted gently with the host. No one would have suspected that only six hours before she'd been lying in Jack's arms in a hotel room. Feigning sleep, she turned onto her side to relive, again and again, the delights of the afternoon.

At 4am she awoke suddenly and found that the thrill, the admiration for her boldness, had been replaced by utter disgust at her behaviour. All those lies. She had liked Alison too and realised that they could have become good friends if circumstances were different.

In the bathroom in the morning her phone beeped by her side (her phone was always by her side now). The promises she'd made to herself in the night fell to nothing as she reached for her mobile as eagerly as any addict for a fix.

Halfway through Carolyn's dinner party, Ali knew that there was something going on between her husband and Sarah Hill. Jack, usually so gregarious in company, was being withdrawn and dull. Sarah was ignoring him to the point of rudeness, acting as though he wasn't in the room at all. Carolyn's husband Trevor, on the other hand, was receiving the full beam of Sarah's attention. His stories were exclaimed over, his weak jokes produced gales of girlish laughter, his hair, his shirt, even his glasses were singled out for extravagant praise.

Ali tried to catch Carolyn's eye to see if she'd noticed anything amiss but Carolyn famously got drunk at her own parties and was now at the stage where she wouldn't have noticed if Sarah had stood on the table and ripped off her dress; in fact, she'd have probably joined in.

Ali waited until they were back at their cottage before confronting her husband. "Is there something going on between you and Sarah Hill?"

"What? What on earth are you talking about? I hardly know the woman."

"I'm not blind, Jack. It's obvious there is something between you."

"Look, you're drunk. You always drink too much when you're with Carolyn. You want to watch that, you know."

He started to walk away. "I'm going to bed," he said.

Ali followed him upstairs, fumbling for her phone. Jack sat heavily on the bed and untied his shoe laces.

"You both thought that you were being so clever ignoring each other tonight but, see, your little tryst at the party last week has all been caught on camera. Look, look!"

Ali pushed her mobile into Jack's face. Reluctantly, he took it off her and thumbed through the photos. He sighed, "All I can see is me talking to a woman at a party. I do that sometimes. I'm sorry if that shocks you. She, Sarah Hill, got a bit tipsy – felt faint she said – and so I helped her outside to get some fresh air. What did you want me to do, let her throw up on Carolyn's Persian rug? She was OK after a while and so I came back in. You and I had a dance, remember?"

Jack continued: "Actually, I think Sarah must have felt a bit embarrassed by it all. She hardly spoke to me tonight; did you notice?"

Ali sat on the bed. Everything that Jack had said sounded reasonable. It could be true; she wanted it to be true.

"And I'm sorry if I was a bit boring tonight darling," Jack said, reaching out to stroke Ali's leg. "I've had such a bloody awful week at the office and now all I want is a quiet weekend with my lovely wife."

Later, curled up in bed with Jack, their long legs intertwined, Ali thought what a fool she was, first with Carolyn and now with her husband. It wasn't like her to be so distrustful and needy. Perhaps she was coming down with something or maybe Jack was right and she was drinking too much and it was making her paranoid.

They didn't do a lot that weekend. They went for long walks along the country lanes, read the papers, completed each other's crosswords and cooked together in the evenings. Jack made his signature dish of Italian chicken with tagliatelle, for which he refused to reveal the recipe but which always necessitated the use of every pan in the kitchen. Ali remembered fondly the first time he'd cooked it, not long after they were married. They only owned two mismatched saucepans and he'd had to run next door to borrow another from their neighbour.

On Sunday evening Jack found a film on TV, which Ali had watched years ago at the cinema and always wanted to see again. It wasn't as good as she'd remembered and, realising that Jack had fallen asleep, she nudged him gently awake and they took their wine glasses up to bed.

A perfect weekend and if Ali had the occasional feeling that Jack was perhaps trying too hard, it was so slight and fleeting that she was hardly aware of it at all.

CHAPTER THREE

Ali's sister, Linda, had the same long legs and green eyes as Ali but her hair was dark and cropped short and, since she'd been a young girl, she'd struggled with her weight. She always wore unusual, brightly coloured clothes that she either made herself or found in charity shops and she accentuated her height by wearing extremely high heels.

For many years Linda had remained single, living and working in North London, where she was employed by the local council. She had many friends and numerous past relationships (which were either short lived or disastrous and often both), which Ali enjoyed vicariously during their weekly telephone conversations.

The sisters, although different in temperament and circumstance, had retained their childhood closeness although Ali, despite being the younger by two years, had gradually adopted the role of the elder sister and nagged Linda about her habits of smoking and sleeping with men she hardly knew.

"But that's the whole point, Ali," Linda would say, sucking heartily on her cigarette. "I've got to get them into bed before I realise I don't like them or I'd never get any sex at all. I never meet anyone even half decent."

But then, one day, she did.

Linda sometimes let out her spare room to make some extra cash and she'd admitted to Ali on the phone that she really fancied her current lodger, Carl. Ali, recalling the tall, skinny youth who'd let her into Linda's house when she last visited and then dashed upstairs without a word, was sceptical.

"Carl? He can't be more than, what, twenty-two?"

"No, he's twenty-nine, so only seventeen years younger than me; that's nothing. Honestly, you wouldn't say a thing if it was the other way round and I was twenty-nine and he was forty-six. I mean, look at Joan Collins and that actress in Thelma and Louise; they had younger men.

Anyway, it's all academic because he's shown no interest in me at all, in that way. Well, he did say he liked my shoes the other morning."

"Your shoes? He's probably gay, Lin."

"I don't think so. He didn't seem to notice Rob when he came round the other night and you know how gorgeous he is and Carl does sometimes, well, look at me in a funny way."

Ali laughed: "He's probably wondering what sort of idiot would combine a green and purple jumper with blue leggings and a tutu," which had been Linda's attire when they last met.

"Don't be so rude. I'll have you know that's my favourite outfit at the moment."

The situation remained unchanged for some months. Linda, at the urging of her friends and colleagues, had signed up with an online dating agency. She'd agreed to go out with a few of the men who'd contacted her but, despite them looking and sounding promising online, the reality had been uniformly disappointing. She'd more or less decided to give up when she was contacted by a man whose profile was witty and whose photo was really quite nice and so she gave it one last try.

It was beyond awful. The man was dressed in a crumpled shirt under an acrylic cardigan and his trousers had stains down the front, which she decided not to look too closely at. He greeted her with a sneer and told her that she didn't look much like her photo, adding, with a leering glance at her chest, that he hoped she had hidden talents. As he smirked at his own joke, she saw that he had nasty grey teeth and at least one missing molar. He was sitting at the bar with a pint of what looked like orange squash in front of him when Linda arrived and, as he made no offer to buy her a drink, she'd had to order her own.

He proceeded to tell her, at great length, about his hobby, which the breeding of Canaries, whilst she tried to make appropriate responses,

"Yes, yes, yellow you say? Wow, amazing." Whoever had written this guy's profile, it certainly wasn't him.

Just when Linda was thinking that she'd fall off her own perch if she listened any longer and beginning to suspect the whole thing was a wind up (she'd kill those bastards at work), he stood up and said, "Look, love, I don't really do fat," and then left.

Carl had found her sitting at the kitchen table, red faced from crying and had taken her hand and led her upstairs to his bedroom where they had remained for the rest of the evening and the whole of the next day. They were married four months later and had been blissfully happy ever since. Canary man's line had become one of their catch phrases; whenever faced with something they didn't like, they'd say, "Look, love, I don't really do" – inserting the offending item – and then collapse into delighted laughter.

CHAPTER FOUR

Ali was busy all of the following week on a major land purchase that had to be completed by Friday, as she and Jack were going on holiday the next day. They'd rented a villa with a private pool in Southern Spain and they'd have seven days together, just the two of them.

The deal Ali was working on was for Drake Developments, who had grown from a partnership of two builders into a successful company. They had taken full advantage of the demand for local housing. Ali's work in purchasing the land and the subsequent conveyancing of the newly built houses, which was carried out by a small team under her supervision, brought a healthy profit into Cassell Brookes and Little and was instrumental in her being made a partner of the firm three years ago.

She had first come across John Drake whilst acting for another client. Mr and Mrs Carlton Greene were an elderly couple who, on the urging of their children, were selling their home with its three acres of garden. With the aid of a planning consultant, recommended by Ali, permission for residential development had been obtained and the house and garden sold to Drake Developments, at a sum which astonished Mr and Mrs Carlton Greene and delighted their offspring.

A meeting was arranged between the parties at which Ali represented the Carlton Greenes, who preferred to remain at home, and a rather pompous young solicitor called Marcus Fielding represented Drake Developments (John Drake, who never remained at home, was also in attendance).

Having sat everyone in the boardroom and offered tea and coffee, Ali handed out copies of the agreed heads of terms and the contracts she had prepared. From the start, Marcus Fielding was determined to be difficult and, in a reedy voice, proposed amendment after amendment to the contracts. Well used to this type of attitude, Ali listened politely to his comments but gradually became aware that Marcus Fielding was not just being argumentative, he was also being obtuse; he didn't actually know what he was talking about.

After Marcus had voiced one particularly inaccurate statement and accompanied it with a knowing smirk to his client, Ali had had enough.

"Surely the effect of the 2011 Act makes your proposed amendment entirely irrelevant, don't you agree Marcus?" Ali asked, smiling sweetly. "And, if we also consider the Court's interpretation of Clause 2A, then we can discount also your changes to pages 4, 5, 7, 8 and, I think, yes, page 12 as well."

It was all too easy after that. She allowed him a couple of minor amendments; she couldn't break the poor man completely and, anyway, she'd learned early on that to concede the unimportant points made it much more likely that you would win the ones that you did want. No one likes to keep on saying no.

A few weeks later John Drake called and asked her to lunch and she'd worked for his company ever since. He swore far too often and he thought nothing of phoning her late in the evening or at weekends but she liked him. He was solid and straightforward, he took her advice and paid his bills on time; the perfect client.

The current deal went well. The seller's solicitor was someone she knew and had worked well with before and, as no last minute issues arose, the papers were signed by Friday afternoon. After everyone had drunk a glass of champagne and left, Ali gave some final instructions to her assistant and to her secretary, Liz, and headed for home. She hadn't started her packing yet and she and Jack were leaving for the airport in the morning.

At the same time that Ali was leaving her office, her sister Linda was sitting in her ancient Volvo with her husband Carl on a stationary M1. They'd been to Leeds to visit

Carl's mother, who was only three years older than Linda, and were on their way back to London.

The radio play they had listened to was over and they had grown tired of inventing stories about their fellow motorists (they'd decided that the bloke in the BMW was big in plumbing accessories and slightly dreading going home to his second wife and two-year-old twins. She'd been his secretary and now he'd got his eye on his new one).

"Shall we pull off at the next services and get a coffee?"

"Good idea. Oh, I think we're starting to move again now."

It was another thirty minutes before they drove into the service station car park. Whilst Linda gathered her bag from the back seat Carl exclaimed, "Isn't that Jack over there? See, talking to that blonde woman."

"Where?" Linda fumbled for her glasses.

To the left of the service station, with its coffee shops and Marks and Spencer, was a small two storey hotel, set back from the car park behind a grassy bank. Jack and a woman had emerged from the hotel's central doorway and now stood, deep in conversation. Jack was holding a briefcase but, apart from that, neither had any luggage.

As Carl and Linda watched, Jack put his case down and pulled the woman towards him. They kissed deeply before pulling apart, only to look at each other and kiss again. Holding hands they turned away from where Carl and Linda watched unnoticed and walked around the back of the hotel.

"Oh my God, Carl. Jack's cheating on Ali. What are we going to do? I can't believe it. Oh poor, poor Ali." Linda started to sob.

Putting his arms around his wife Carl tried to be optimistic, "Look, she could be a colleague who's just had some bad news; maybe her hamster has died or something."

Carl could always make Linda laugh but not this time.

"Well, I'm going to bloody well find out what he's up to. I'm calling his mobile right now."

"You don't have to, Lin, look, he's coming back towards us."

Jack, alone now and holding his car keys in his hand, was walking right in front of their car. His smile, when he first saw Linda, quickly faded and they were all aware of the panic in his eyes before he covered it with a mask of pleased surprise.

"Linda! And Carl too. How long have you, um, I mean what a coincidence. Have you been up to Leeds?"

Linda had by now stopped crying and her voice was icily calm: "We saw Jack. We saw you and that woman kissing and don't think we don't know what you were both doing in that cheap hotel. You disappoint me, Jack. I thought you'd have more class than that. So, how long have you been cheating on my sister?"

A family group, all clutching enormous paper cups of coffee, stood nearby, openly listening to the conversation.

"Look," said Carl. "Why don't we go and get a coffee and talk about this?"

Linda felt unaccountably annoyed at Carl's reasonable tone. Surely, he should have punched Jack to the ground by now. She satisfied herself with giving Jack's briefcase a kick (it was Italian leather, a present from Ali) and, feeling marginally better, followed the men into the coffee shop.

Carl, for once, took the lead in the conversation: "Look, mate, it's pretty obvious that you've just spent the afternoon shagging some woman. That maybe none of our business but it affects Ali and so it affects us too. I'm sure you see that."

At the mention of his wife's name, Jack went white. "Please, please don't tell Ali. It was a moment of madness, a one off. I've never done anything like this before."

"The thing is, Jack," said Linda, "I have to think of my sister. I'd want to know if Carl was fucking someone else and, if Ali knew, she'd definitely tell me."

Linda paused and drank some of her coffee before

19

continuing: "However, I'm not going to tell her."

"You're not. Oh thank God!"

"No, you are, Jack. You're going to tell her yourself tonight. If she hasn't called me by tomorrow morning, then I will tell her myself."

Linda's one concession, looking at the face of the man who'd made her sister so happy, with whom she'd shared so many family celebrations and who was the father of her adored niece, was to agree that she wouldn't tell Ali that she knew. She'd let Ali believe that Jack, full of remorse, had wanted to tell her himself. If Ali knew that Jack's hand had been forced then she may never forgive him. This way, there may just be a chance.

"It was just a one off, Jack? With this woman?"

"Oh yes, a one off. I'll never do it again. I swear to you."

CHAPTER FIVE

The taxi turned left and started to climb up a narrow winding road. Ahead, Ali could see a cluster of whitewashed houses and, rising above terracotta roofs, a church steeple. The driver came to a halt in a square and, winding down his window, shouted to a group of men who were sat under the tattered awning of a bar.

"Hombres, Casa Olivia, donde esta?"

Ali realised that the taxi driver was asking for directions to the villa and hoped that the local men would know; it was impossibly hot in the stationary car.

There followed an impossibly long discussion with much arm waving but finally the driver appeared satisfied and he edged the taxi up a sharp incline. Coming to the brow of a hill, the road veered to the left and they dropped down into a smaller square, lined with a few shops, whose dark interiors were hidden behind beaded curtains. A few yards further on they arrived at an iron gate set in a high white wall. Through the car window Ali could see a slate plaque with the words "Casa Olivia" and, peeling her legs off the shabby vinyl seat, stepped out of the car.

Once the taxi had driven away, leaving Ali and her suitcase in the dusty street, she felt her spirits, already low, drop even further and had a wild desire to call the taxi driver back and ask him to drive her to a hotel, preferably in a city centre, anywhere but this seemingly deserted place. There was supposed to be someone from the rental agency to meet her but, apart from a few hot looking dogs lying in the shade, there was no one to be seen.

There was no bell or knocker on the wall and she tried calling through the gate, "Hello. Hola, is anyone there?" but nobody answered.

Ali rang the agency number again but just received a recorded message. She'd just decided to leave her suitcase where it was and walk back to the bar when she heard a scooter coming down the hill towards her. A young boy, very tanned and dressed in denim shorts and a white T-shirt, jumped off his bike and smiled at her.

"Alison, yes? Sorry I'm a bit late, I'd forgotten the keys and had to go back. Anyway, I'm Elena, welcome to Compesita."

Ali now saw that the boy was actually a young woman in her mid-twenties, small and slender with a long straight nose and white even teeth. Her light brown hair was just visible underneath a baseball cap. Elena pulled a set of keys from the pocket of her shorts and, opening the iron gates, waved for Ali to follow.

"You look a bit wrecked. I expect you had to get up early. I'll just show you where everything is and then I guess you'll want to crash out. Are you on your own? I thought there'd be two of you."

"No, not two of us. Just me, I'm afraid. My husband couldn't get away in the end. Something came up at work."

That was the story she and Jack had decided upon at the end of that awful night. *My God*, Ali thought, it was less than twenty-four hours ago. Once she'd insisted that she wanted to go on holiday by herself, she told Jack that she didn't care what other people would think; he could tell them whatever he liked.

"But, Ali, what about Lucy? Are you ready to tell Lucy everything? Can't we wait at least until you get back?"

Ali knew that what he meant was "why don't we wait and see if you do decide to leave me for good before we start telling everyone", but, thinking of her daughter, she agreed to say, if anyone asked, that a last minute crisis had occurred in Jack's office and, rather than cancel their holiday, Ali had gone to Spain on her own.

When she'd got home from work on Friday evening, she'd felt so happy; seven days without clients, nothing to do except lie in the sun, read, eat delicious meals and be with Jack. He was later home than she expected but, as soon as she heard his key in the lock, she ran downstairs holding a pair of men's shorts in each hand.

"Hey, holiday boy. Look what I got you. How trendy are these! They had a sale on at that shop you like in town. I've nearly finished the packing. I may, just possibly, need to put some of my shoes and things in your case. We can make room if we take out your... hey, what's wrong?"

Ali looked in concern at Jack's stricken face: "I was only joking about the shoes."

"We need to talk, Ali." Jack sat down on the stair and pulled Ali's arm so that they sat together, side by side. There in the hallway, looking not at Ali but straight ahead, Jack told her about Sarah Hill. He said that he'd met her at the golf club with her husband, that she'd somehow got hold of his mobile number and had called him a few days later, that they'd met and it had gone on from there. In a flat, unemotional voice, he said that he'd slept with her twice.

Jack turned to look at Ali for the first time, his voice now beginning to crack, "I'm so, so sorry, darling. It was madness. It was as though I'd been drugged or something and now I realise what I've done, I had to tell you. This is the hardest thing I've ever, ever done. I just hope that you can see how sorry I am and that you can forgive me."

Ali had been listening to Jack's words as though in a trance. Realising that he'd stopped speaking and was now looking at her pleadingly, she stood up.

"So, I was right. When you said that I was drunk and paranoid after that dinner party, you made me feel as if there was something wrong with me and all the time you were fucking that bitch. Oh, God, I think I'm going to be sick. No, no, leave me alone. Get away from me," she said.

Ali shook off Jack's hand and ran through the kitchen into the garden. She walked down a gravel path and sat in the dusk on a stone bench. She could see the lights of the cottage; Jack had not followed her out.

Her thoughts were crashing around in her head. It suddenly felt as though Jack was a complete stranger to her. The future that she'd always assumed they'd spend together had been destroyed, to be replaced by bleakness and despair. She was hit by a sudden and utter fury. What an absolute bastard he was. She'd done nothing but give him love. She'd always supported him, listened to his problems at work, raved over his pathetic attempts at cooking. Why didn't he just say no to that woman. What did he see in the skinny blonde cow anyway.

As suddenly as it had occurred, Ali's rage left her and she slumped on the bench, shivering and wretched. Jack walked down the path towards her and put his hand gently on her shoulder: "Come back into the house, please, love. We can talk. I'll tell you anything you want to know. I'm so sorry. I never meant to hurt you."

"I just can't believe it, Linda. I know I've sometimes felt a bit jealous when other women flirt with Jack, but I never actually thought that he'd cheat on me. I thought we were special. I thought he adored me."

Jack and Ali had talked for over an hour. She'd insisted on hearing every detail. Jack had admitted that it had been going on for weeks and that they had slept together, not just twice, but several times, meeting in hotels or at her house. Finally, Ali could bear it no longer and she told Jack to go away and leave her on her own. They were both in tears when he left and Ali sat for a while, doing nothing, just staring at the kitchen wall, before calling her sister.

"I can't believe it's true either, Ali. Has he said why he did it?"

"Oh, some crap about his being under pressure at work, all the young guys gunning for his job. Then he said that I'm always so wrapped up in my work, as if it were my fault."

"Well I'm sure he didn't mean it that way, Ali. It's probably some sort of midlife crisis; this woman has flattered his ego. Obviously, she's a complete bitch to go after someone else's husband. Is she married? Does her husband know?"

"She's married alright. They live in the village. I nearly went straight round there and knocked on her door, but I wasn't sure I could do it without bursting into tears and I didn't want to give her the satisfaction."

"Jack did tell you about it, Ali, didn't he? I mean, he didn't have to do that. He said it is definitely over?"

"Yes, he said it meant nothing to him and he cried. I've never seen him cry before. Oh, Linda," Ali started sobbing again, "I'm so angry with him. I thought we had this perfect life. I used to feel sorry for other couples who sniped at each other; Jack and I hardly ever argued. But now I don't see how I can trust him again. I keep imagining him in bed with her. I see the two of them together; his face looking down at her, the same way he looks at me. Oh God, I don't think I can bear it. I don't know what to do."

"Look, Als, you've had a dreadful shock. You can't decide anything at the moment. Why don't you come and stay with us for a while?"

"We were supposed to be flying to Spain in the morning. I've just been packing his bloody clothes. I was looking forward to the holiday so much."

"Well, why don't you go? Go on your own and have some time by yourself to think it all through. You can lie in the sun, read loads of trashy books and leave Jack to think of all the ways he can make it up to you. I would come with you myself but it's manic at work at the mo and I don't think I can get any time off." Ali heard Linda light another cigarette. "And, if you do decide that it's all over between you, at least you'll be looking brown and gorgeous when you end it. What do you think?"

When Jack came back an hour later, Ali coolly told him that she was going to Spain without him. He wasn't to come or to even contact her while she was away and that she'd talk to him when she got back; when she'd had time to think things through.

"Well, yes, of course, if that's what you want, darling. I'll run you to the airport."

"It's not what I want, Jack. What I want is for this to have never happened and, don't bother, I'll get a taxi to the airport, I'll order it now. I'd like you to leave please. I don't care where you go. I don't want to look at your face any longer."

Ali went into the sitting room to find the number of the airport taxi firm. When she'd finished the call, she looked up to see Jack in the hall holding his gym bag. He started to walk towards her but she turned away and said, "Just go, Jack." After she'd heard his car reversing down the drive, Ali sat on the sofa, put her head in her hands and wept with a ferocity she'd never experienced before. Her body shook with every gulping cry and she slumped sideways, staining the silk cushions with her tears. When she finally got up and switched on a lamp in the darkening room, she didn't recognise herself in the mirror. It wasn't just that her eyes were red and swollen, they no longer had their usual confident, slightly amused expression. The face which stared back at her belonged to someone else, someone who was lost, defeated and afraid.

CHAPTER SIX

For the first three days Ali didn't leave the villa. Unable to sleep at night, she wandered around the house or stood outside on the terrace, doing nothing, just listening to the sounds of the evening. Often, during the day, she'd close the shutters in the bedroom and sleep fitfully, only to wake up and find that she'd been crying.

When she'd arrived, Ali had sent text messages to Linda, Lucy and Jack to say that she'd got there safely. To Lucy she'd also written that the villa was fab and added a smiley face. To Jack, she'd reiterated that he was not to call her.

After the messages had been sent, Ali switched off her phone and threw it in her case, which lay open but unpacked on the bedroom floor. Her bright holiday clothes taunted her with their false promise of happiness.

On the fourth day, she awoke and, going into the kitchen, realised that she'd run out of bottled water, coffee and, indeed, just about everything. The rental agency had supplied the villa with various items (a welcome pack, Elena had called it), including bottled water, instant coffee, milk, bread and cheese. There had also been a bottle of red wine but Ali feared to open it, thinking that if she started drinking she may never stop. Everything else she'd now eaten or drunk, making herself toasted cheese sandwiches for breakfast, lunch and dinner.

She showered, put on a red sleeveless dress and flat sandals and, for the first time since she'd arrived, stepped out of the villa walls. The June sun was hot and by the time Ali had walked up the hill to the little square, she was out of breath. Inside the general store it was cool and dark and, when her eyes had grown accustomed to the gloom, she saw that, despite its size, the shop was surprisingly well stocked.

Taking a basket, Ali wandered around the shelves, collecting water, ground coffee, two bottles of pale Rose wine, olives and almonds. Seeing some French beans, she added a handful of those with some potatoes, half a dozen eggs and a tin of tuna, thinking that she could make a Salad Nicoise for lunch and realising that she felt hungry for the first time in days. At the last minute she placed a bar of dark chocolate and a bottle of Vodka in her basket; an orange tree overhung the villa wall and she'd pick a few oranges and have an aperitif before lunch.

There were quite a few people in the shop now, all seemingly local villagers known to the shop keeper and everyone was standing in front of the counter, talking at once. Ali held her basket, which was extremely heavy by now, and hung back, waiting for a lull in the conversation so that she could pay. The shop keeper, without pausing in her conversation, gestured to Ali to place her basket on the counter.

Ali tried to remember the Spanish word for bread. Pan, was it, or was that French?

"Er, pan, senora?"

Pointing across the square to the bread shop, the shopkeeper nodded encouragingly at Ali.

Having paid and lugged her shopping bags across the square, Ali bought a flat round loaf and started back down the hill. However, the large bottle of water was heavy and, as she struggled to get a better grip on the carrier bags, the handle of one broke, spilling potatoes into the road. The sense of achievement that she had felt buying the shopping evaporated and, missing Jack, she bit her lip and felt tears come into her eyes.

"Oh dear, do you need some help? Can I give you a lift?"

A battered Peugeot had stopped beside her and a man, very tanned with grey, slightly receding curly hair, leaned out of the window.

"Well," said Ali, "I'm only going a little way down the hill, Casa Olivia? But the wretched carrier bag has split."

By now the man had unfolded himself from the car. He was extremely tall, at least 6' 3'', and, putting her shopping on the back seat, he said, "Hop in then."

It only took a minute or so to reach the villa but the man (Ali didn't even know his name) insisted on carrying her bags inside. He refused her offer of a drink and sped off down the hill. When she'd put the shopping away and had a swim in the villa's tiny pool, Ali quickly and rather guiltily raided the neighbour's orange tree and sat in the shade on the terrace with an absolutely enormous Vodka and orange juice.

"What on earth is the matter, darling? You're as white as a sheet. It was only the woman from the charity shop asking if we'd got anything for them. I told her that it was no good coming to us as my wife always says she's got absolutely nothing in her wardrobe."

Chris Hill started to laugh at his own joke but then looked at his wife in concern: "You do look peaky, love. I know, let's go out somewhere for the day tomorrow. Jack Jones has cancelled our game tomorrow, so I'm free all day."

Sarah started, "Jack? Did he call the house? When?"

"No, he rang me this morning, well, left a message on my mobile actually. I expect something came up or perhaps he's decided to take his wife out for the day as well."

"Actually, Chris, I do have a bit of a headache. I think I'll go upstairs and lie down."

Ever since Jack had called her on Friday afternoon, Sarah had been full of dread. They'd only parted outside the hotel an hour earlier and she'd just got back home. Seeing his number on her caller ID, she'd smiled, congratulating herself; she'd clearly got under his skin. Instead, he'd said, quite coldly, that it was over between them. They'd been seen at the hotel by his wife's sister and she was insisting that he tell his wife that he'd been sleeping with someone else or the she would. He had told Sarah that he was going home to tell his wife now and feared she'd never forgive him. He then rang off. He called back a few seconds later to say that it was best if Sarah didn't call him again and then he cut Sarah off for the second time.

Sarah had gone into the kitchen and poured herself a large gin and tonic. She felt utterly humiliated but, to her surprise, she wasn't devastated. If anything, she felt a sense of relief. It was almost as though her feelings for Jack were dependent on his for her. What she'd really loved was that he'd found her irresistible; well, clearly no more.

She drained her glass and reached for the gin bottle when another thought struck her; what if Jack's wife told Chris? Came round to the house and caused a scene; marched into the golf club or waylaid Chris at his office. Kind, loyal Chris would never forgive her. What a fool she'd been; what an absolute bloody fool.

Ali looked around and for a few minutes couldn't remember where she was. Her mouth was dry and she was lying on top of her bed at the villa. The shutters were open but outside it was dark. Pushing herself up off the bed, she turned on the lamp and looked at her watch, ten o'clock. Her red dress was in a heap on the floor and, on the bedside table beside an empty glass, her mobile phone lay blinking. Her phone, what was that doing there? She'd left it in her suitcase surely?

Slowly, memories of the afternoon came back to her. She'd drink her Vodka and orange juice, had another one and then several straight Vodkas. She couldn't remember lying on the bed but she did now recall getting her phone from her case and, oh no, calling Jack.

Ali forced herself to look at her phone. The sent box showed four messages, all to Jack:

'You don't know what you're missing. I've met loads of people. Off to a party now – yayyy!'

'Do you have any idea what you've done to me, you piece of shit. I hate you!'

'What did I do wrong, Jack? I thought we were so

happy.'

'Lust wish yo were now ccc.'

The inbox showed three messages. Before she could bring herself to read them, Ali made herself a pot of coffee and a piece of toast and went to sit in the living room.

The first message was from Linda:

"Shagged any hot Spaniards yet – LOL. Thinking of you, sis. Call me anytime. Love you xx'

The next two messages were from Jack:

'Glad you're having a good time, darling. I miss you and I love you so much.'

'Are you still at the party, Ali? Is there anyone there with you? Call me please, I'm worried about you.'

Looking at the call log, Ali saw there were seven missed calls, all from Jack.

The landline was answered on the first ring: "Jack, it's me Ali."

"Ali, thank God. Where are you? Are you still at the party?"

"There was no party, Jack; well, a party of one maybe. I was, well, I made it all up. Anyway, I thought I'd better let you know that I'm OK; fine actually. I didn't want you dashing to the airport or anything."

"No, I'm just at home catching up on some work. I miss you."

There was a pause, then Ali said, "Bye, Jack," and rang off, before she found herself saying that she missed him too. Although she was relieved that Jack wasn't on his way to see her, she felt slightly resentful that he hadn't been more spontaneous. How very sensible of him to wait at home for her to call.

Having slept for several hours Ali was now wide awake. She got another coffee and found a pen and paper. She'd try and make some sense of the thoughts which had been swirling around in her head since Friday night. If she wrote everything down, she could treat it like she would a problem at work; apply some logic to the emotional

31

morass. She'd start by detailing what had happened – the facts – and hopefully this may lead to why it had happened – the motive – and finally what her response should be – the judgement.

After a few hours Ali put down her pen, stretched out on the sofa and closed her eyes. When she opened them again it was morning, the room filled with brilliant light. She decided to go for a walk, explore the village and maybe have some breakfast. She showered and changed and, grabbing her sunglasses and a hat, shut the door behind her.

Ali followed the route that the taxi driver had taken on Saturday morning, but in reverse. Up the hill into the small square with the general store and bakery and then down into the larger, main square, where there were three bars. There was the one with the tattered awning, which the taxi had stopped outside the day she arrived; the same group of men appeared not to have moved. Another similar bar was directly opposite and there was a smaller one in the far corner, with little round thatched umbrellas over mismatched tables and chairs.

Ali walked over to the corner bar and sat, a little self-consciously, at the nearest table. Having ordered orange juice and a tostada, uncomfortably aware of the interest she had drawn from the men opposite (some of whom had turned their chairs around in order to see her more clearly), she took out her notes from last night and began to read.

The facts she skipped; she had re-run them in her head too many times already. The motivation – the reason why – seemed to be the key. If she understood why Jack had had the affair, then she may be able to judge whether or not it would happen again and if she could trust him.

It was clear to Ali by now that she still loved him. It was impossible to stop loving someone overnight. She also thought that she could forgive him. Trust, however, was altogether something more.

Having finished her breakfast and done enough soul searching, Ali wanted to see more of Compesita. She climbed the narrow streets which wound up beyond the square, peering into the gloomy interiors of the cottages lining the roads and smiling at little black clad old ladies. The church, whose spire she'd seen on her first day, was at the very top of the village, surrounded by another large square. The town hall was here too with a noticeboard advertising, in English, forthcoming events, Flamenco classes and Spanish lessons. On one handwritten card someone called Brian was asking for a partner for golf and Ali reached into her bag for a pen to jot down the number, before remembering that Jack wasn't with her.

Ali could just see the white wall of Casa Olivia from where she stood and thought that, if she made her way down behind the church, she should come round in a circle back to her villa. This part of the village was less densely packed, the houses set in their own gardens. The flowers were lovely but Ali soon gave up trying to name them; Jack was the gardener in their family.

There was one garden which was particularly beautiful; the house too. It was clearly quite old and was long and low, single storey apart from a sort of tower at one end. Ali went a little closer to the entrance to get a better view when she noticed, to her embarrassment, a man was standing just inside the garden holding a watering can.

"Hello, it's Olivia isn't it? Well, I didn't get your name the other day and so Ronny and I call you that." It was the man in the Peugeot, who'd helped with her shopping.

"My name is Alison; Ali. Not as pretty as Olivia, I'm afraid. Sorry I was snooping, but your house and garden are both so lovely."

"Well, you must come and have a look round sometime. Ronny's out at the moment but why don't you come and have a drink with us this evening, say about six?"

Ali wasn't sure that she was up to other people's company, let alone drinking but she couldn't think of a reasonable excuse and so agreed to go.

The Peugeot man, whose name was Alan, had offered

33

to collect her but she said that she was fine to walk. Indeed, on the way back, she found a set of old stone steps that led to an alley at the side of the bakers and so it wasn't far at all.

At five past six, dressed in one of her new holiday outfits (they'd looked less sad, somehow, when she'd made herself unpack), Ali arrived at Alan and Ronny's house. The front door was open and she could hear music – Chet Baker – one of Jack's favourites. She was just about to call out when a woman came down the hall and, holding out both of her hands said, "You must be the lovely Alison Olivia. Welcome to Cortijo Viejo. I'm Ronny."

When Alan had mentioned Ronny earlier, Ali had assumed he'd be a man. She'd pictured Ronnie Corbett, small and dapper to Alan's towering untidiness. She'd nearly called Linda, who would have been delighted in the scenario and have invented a whole biography of the two men's lives. However, she knew that her sister was in touch with Jack and, if she told him that Ali was off to a drinks party, Jack, with some justification, would think that she'd made it up again; even worse, that she was now creating detailed descriptions of her fantasy characters.

The Ronny before her was extremely feminine. She was small and very slim with short, feathery dark hair and the most amazing cheekbones Ali had ever seen. She was probably in her early fifties but she was the sort of woman who'd look beautiful when she was eighty. She wore white linen trousers and a pale grey shirt which matched her eyes.

Ali handed over one of her bottles of wine and followed Ronny into the kitchen. Putting Ali's wine on the counter, Ronny said, "Let's have a Tinto De Verano; do you know it? It's very light, just lemonade with red wine and Martini Rosso. Now, would you like to see around the cortijo? Alan is just changing, he'll be down in a minute."

The cortijo, an old Spanish farmhouse, was lovely. Uneven white walls set off the polished wooden floors.

Large sofas were interspersed with pieces of antique furniture and there were massive mirrors and ceramic jugs of flowers everywhere. The tower had three storeys, with the kitchen on the ground floor, a large bedroom above and, at the top, an art studio with magnificent views to the sea in the far distance.

In the studio Ali turned away from the window with some reluctance. Canvasses were stacked up against every wall and a paint splattered easel displayed a work in progress. Every canvass, without exception, was absolutely terrible and all, Ali realised, were the work of Ronny. Ali had been puzzled by the hideous paintings which hung on every wall downstairs and which seemed so incongruous in the tasteful rooms. It wasn't only that they lacked any artistic merit, it was the subject matter too. There were grimy faced children with tears on their cheeks, a sad looking matador and a group of goats herded by what appeared to be a nine foot boy.

The picture on the easel showed a woman in peasant costume holding an urn on her head. The urn was easily as big as she was but what caused rising hysteria in Ali was the woman's face; she looked exactly like a rather cross Prince Philip. Ali had to press her lips together to stop herself from laughing out loud.

Ronny was looking at her expectantly.

"Mmmm," Ali murmured. "Mmmm." She was still reluctant to open her mouth and, instead, executed a sort of twirl, extending her arms in what she hoped was a convincing mime for "these paintings are beyond words".

She was saved by Alan, who bounded up the stairs and, gazing at Ronny adoringly, said to Ali, "What a talent. Isn't she just astonishing?"

"That's the word I was looking for, Alan, astonishing."

Alan made them another drink and they carried them into the garden. Ronny made tactful enquiries into Ali's reasons for travelling alone and she found herself telling the couple a little of her situation.

"If you love one another enough, Alison Olivia, then

35

you will work it out." Ronny reached for Alan's hand. "We had to overcome many, many difficulties to be together, but here we are."

When Alan suggested to Ronny that she bring her guitar into the garden – "she plays as well as she paints" – Ali made her excuses and left, saying that she felt a little tired.

Earlier, on hearing that Ali had not yet been down to the coast, Alan had offered to drive her there the next morning.

"There is a local bus but it's rather erratic. If you come down with me, you can get a taxi back. It's only about twenty minutes away."

Before walking back Ali had thanked her hosts for a lovely evening; to her surprise she had really enjoyed herself.

CHAPTER SEVEN

Whenever Ali had a problem, the first person she would call was her friend Emma. They'd been best friends since school and had shared a flat together before Ali met and married Jack. Although it was now resolved, when Lucy was born there had been a tension in their friendship for a while. Ali, struggling with the massive change to her life when she'd given birth, had been very hurt when Emma, instead of rallying around and being supportive, rarely visited or even called. Ali first assumed that Emma had found her boring, now that she was the mother of a young child but, on the occasions that Ali took Lucy to Emma's London flat, Emma was her old self and clearly enchanted by Lucy, so it was all very strange.

Emma invariably made excuses when Ali invited her round. On the rare times she did come, she never stayed for very long and never overnight. Ali had often spoken to Jack about it but he'd said that he was as puzzled as she was. He said that maybe Emma just needed some more time to adjust to Ali's new circumstances and Ali was touched to notice that Jack would usually arrange to leave the two women together during Emma's visits, often looking after Lucy so that they could go shopping or out for lunch.

Jack also encouraged Ali to go and stay with Emma in London and, over the years, they'd even had several short trips abroad together, including a riotous weekend in Istanbul when Ali had managed to lose one of her shoes in a restaurant and they'd stayed out so late on their last evening that they'd missed their flight home.

Ali had waited until she arrived in Spain before she called Emma to tell her what had happened. She wasn't sure why she hadn't phoned her friend straight away but Ali realised that she felt vaguely ashamed at having to admit to her single friend that the marriage she had so often spoken about with such certainty, smugness even, was less than perfect.

Emma had been wonderful. She hadn't offered any advice, other than to tell her to look after herself as well as she could, but had listened to Ali's repetitive words and had called and sent her text messages throughout each day. Every morning and every evening Emma's voice would be the first and last thing Ali would hear and through her misery she recognised her friend's love.

During the drive to the beach the next morning Alan told Ali that Ronny was sorry that she couldn't be with them but that she always meditated in the mornings. When Ali suggested that she did seem to have a very calm presence, Alan readily agreed: "You noticed that, did you? It was one of the first things I thought when I met her. I've loved her from that very moment and I've never stopped."

Ali thought how amazing it was to hear a man talking so lovingly of his wife; it was really starting to get on her nerves.

"It hasn't been easy for her, you see. My wife, my first wife, died. She'd been ill for a long time. I met Ronny quite soon after and we were married within three months. My children, all grown up of course, have never accepted Ronny or forgiven me. I don't mind what they think of me but if they can't be civil to Ronny then they are not welcome in our lives."

They drove on in silence. Ali wondered what she'd do if she ever had to choose between Jack and Lucy; surely you'd choose your child, wouldn't you? What a sad situation. She couldn't help thinking that Alan's feelings for Ronny were so intense because he had channelled his love for his family into one person.

The Peugeot struggled up a hill and then the road dropped and Ali could see the sea quite clearly. There was a sandy, crescent shaped beach with steep cliffs at either end. Alan pulled over at the side of the road. Between the road and the beach was a paved walkway running the length of the sands. A number of bars, shops and restaurants were dotted along the walkway and, although it was quite early, there were a number of people strolling about or sitting under umbrellas on the beach.

Alan pointed to a nearby bar, La Bota. "There are usually a few taxis outside there; ask the waiter to call one for you if there aren't. Ronny and I usually go to one of the places at the far end for lunch, they're all good but the Bella Vista is our favourite. Well, have a good day."

Ali waved him off and then set out to explore the beach. She went to the end of the walkway and decided that she'd have lunch at the very last restaurant which had tables facing the sea and a blackboard promising a variety of freshly caught local fish.

She spent the rest of the morning lying on the beach, swimming in the sea when she got too hot. She tried to read her book but her thoughts kept drifting back to Jack and Sarah. Bored with them and with her own self-pity, Ali distracted herself by watching the other people around her. They were mainly Spanish families but she also heard French and German voices and enjoyed a conversation between two very tanned women with strong Liverpool accents: "So, what did youse say to that?"

"I said I'm not having it. I haven't gone to the trouble of buying a Marks and Sparks lasagne and putting on my strapless bra to be insulted in me own home."

Unfortunately, a Spanish family began a very noisy ball game and so Ali never found out what the insult had been.

Ali had a late lunch and it was nearly four o'clock when she returned to doze on her sunbed. Something rather nice had happened in the restaurant and she couldn't help smiling as she thought of it. During the meal, men selling various items; watches, sunglasses, flowers, wandered between the tables and, although seemingly tolerated by the waiters, they were mainly waved away by the diners. As a group of elderly Spanish men rose to leave, one of them came over to Ali's table and, with a gallant bow, handed her a single red rose.

The waiter, who had clearly been distressed by Ali's

solo status and gently attentive throughout her lunch, delightedly brought her a large brandy.

"La casa invita senorita (on the house)." Sipping the brandy Ali remembered with pleasure that senorita meant girl; how wonderfully gallant the Spanish men were.

Just after six o'clock, Ali gathered her things and walked back to La Bota. There was a taxi outside but no driver and so she went inside the bar to enquire.

"Taxi?"

The barman pointed to a man sitting at the end of the bar eating a plate of calamari.

"Sí, senora, diez minutos."

The inside of the bar was cool and so Ali sat at a table and ordered a glass of wine whilst she waited for the driver to finish his meal. The ten minutes stretched to twenty as the driver lingered over coffee and the bar filled up as people came in from the beach. A group of three men scanned the room and then walked over to Ali's table and asked if they could join her. Ali couldn't help overhearing their conversation. They'd been scuba diving and the outing appeared to have been an utter disaster. Ali found herself smiling at some of their comments and, encouraged, they started to ask her about her day. When one of the men offered her a drink, it seemed unfriendly to refuse and, as their stories continued, Ali hardly noticed the taxi driver leaving the bar.

She was halfway through her third glass of wine (she'd insisted on buying a round of drinks) when she realised that she was feeling a little drunk. She'd not long before had wine with her lunch, as well as a brandy and she decided that, once she'd finished her drink, she'd go outside and see if the taxi was there; the fresh air would do her good. However, when she rose to leave, one of the men said that he'd go and check for her. He came back shaking his head.

"I just saw him driving off; missed him by seconds. Oh well, another drink I think. Same again all round?"

Although Ali asked for water, a glass of wine was placed in front of her. She thought of the empty villa and the long, no doubt sleepless night ahead of her and wondered why she was so keen to go back there.

"Cheers, guys. Now, where would you say is the best place in the world to go diving?"

It was another hour before Ali finally pushed herself off her chair and, waving goodbye to her drinking companions, made her way unsteadily outside. A taxi was waiting in the road but, as she went towards it, she saw another couple approaching from the opposite direction. By now Ali really wanted to get back to the villa. She started to run but felt someone grab her arm and, turning, she saw that it was one of the men from the bar.

"Hey, not so fast, gorgeous. You haven't said goodbye properly," and he lunged forward and put his mouth over hers. His breath stank of beer and cigarettes and Ali struggled to get free but his grip on her arm only intensified.

She managed to twist to one side and shouted, "Get off me, get lost!"

"Don't be like that, love, come on."

The man now held her other arm and pulled her towards him.

"Oh there you are, darling. We've been waiting for you. Quickly, hop in."

A couple were sitting in the back of the taxi and gesturing to her from the open rear door. Ali's attacker turned to see who was speaking and she took the opportunity to break free from him and ran to the taxi. As it pulled away she could see his snarling face through the rear window.

The couple looked at her in concern and the woman asked, "Are you OK? I hope we weren't interfering but you didn't look as though you were having much fun."

Ali was breathing hard and it took her a minute before she could trust herself to speak without bursting into tears.

41

"Yes, I'm fine now but thank you for coming to my rescue. I'd got myself into a bit of a tricky situation. I'm normally very sensible, you must think I'm awful."

At this, Ali did start to cry but the woman calmly continued to talk, telling Ali about their day; where they'd had lunch and the souvenirs they had bought and so Ali was able to bring herself under control and to speak normally.

The couple were very kind and insisted on dropping Ali right outside her villa. They said they were staying in another village nearby; Ali hoped that this was true and that they hadn't gone miles out of their way. They wouldn't let her pay the fare either, which only made her feel worse.

Ali felt certain that she wouldn't be able to sleep that night but she did, waking early the next morning feeling surprisingly buoyant, although her aching head reminded her of how much she'd drunk the previous day. She now saw, with absolute clarity, that she wanted her life with Jack to continue. She had never been in any doubt that she still loved him but now she was sure that she wanted to forgive him and move on. Ali knew that it wouldn't be easy but she wanted it to work and that would make anything possible.

Today was her last day at the villa. Ali planned to do nothing very much; pack, go for a walk and maybe go to one of the bars in the square for a meal before an early night. Ronny had told her that there was a little market in Compesita on Friday mornings and she set off to find it, wanting to buy presents for Lucy and the girls in the office.

Ali found the market quite easily strung along the narrow streets near to the main square. The stalls all appeared to sell either vegetables or enormous lacy bras but there was one where a young dreadlocked couple were selling handmade jewellery and Ali bought beaded bracelets for the office girls and a pair of delicate silver earrings for Lucy. She also bought herself a white linen skirt and, from a sad old man with very few items on display, a dusty bottle of homemade wine to give to Jack. *I expect it will poison him*, she thought cheerfully.

It was amazing how much better she felt now that she had decided what to do about the future. Uncertainty was a very stressful state of mind and Ali resolved to be more decisive in all areas of her life in the future. She considered calling Jack but thought that she would wait until she got home and they could talk face to face.

In the afternoon Ali finished her packing, swam and had a siesta. Just after seven, she put on her new white skirt and a navy sleeveless top and walked up to the square. The corner bar appeared to be closed and so she chose the larger of the other two bars and sat outside under the awning. As it was early, the bar was almost empty and her order of tortilla and an abstemious bottle of sparkling water was taken quickly.

Ali was sipping her water when a taxi drew into the square and the couple from last night stepped out. Ali hoped that they wouldn't see her and would go over to the other bar; she felt so ashamed about her stupidity the previous day. And what would they think if they saw her sitting alone in a bar again, thank God she was only drinking water.

She was studying the menu with fierce concentration when they walked over to her table. "Hi there. We thought it was you. How are you? May we join you or are you waiting for someone?"

The couple were smiling expectantly at her. They looked remarkably alike; both had light brown wavy hair and hazel eyes. The husband had a beard, however, which luckily his wife did not. Ali didn't normally like beards much but it suited this man.

"Please do join me," Ali said. "I'm on my own tonight. No male companions, as you can see."

They didn't refer to the previous night again. The

conversation flowed easily and Ali enjoyed their company. The husband she thought very attractive. He wasn't very tall but had a compact, muscular body and his eyes were expressive and intelligent. He had a dry sense of humour and their table rang with laughter as the evening wore on. As dusk fell, the lights around the square glimmered with a soft yellow glow and the bar, so ordinary during the day, appeared to be romantic and special.

"How long have you two been together?" Ali asked.

They both laughed: "About forty years," the woman said. Well, forty-one actually. It's Paul's birthday next week."

"Jan's my big sister." Paul raised his eyebrows. "Oh God, I can't believe that you thought we were married. You really must stop kissing me on the lips Jan."

"Oh, ha-ha; I'm more likely to wring your neck," and she proceeded to do so.

Jan and Paul were staying in the next village in a house owned by Jan and her husband.

"He doesn't like it here in the summer, it's too hot and so Paul and I often come out together. We're both teachers, well, Paul's a lecturer and so we have lots of holiday time to use up."

"Yes, we come from a long line of teachers; both our parents were. I wanted to be a heart surgeon but they wouldn't hear of it."

"The schools haven't broken up yet, have they?" asked Ali.

"No, but I only work part time and Paul's on a bit of a sabbatical at the moment" – Jan paused and glanced at her brother – "and so we decided to come out for a few days."

Jan gestured to the waiter for another glass of wine (Paul, Ali noticed, had, like her, only drunk water) and Ali got up to leave, explaining that she was flying home the next day. Walking back to Casa Olivia, Ali realised that, for the first time in a week, she felt happy; happy and optimistic about the future.

CHAPTER EIGHT

Ali's flight home was on time and by early afternoon she was back home. Jack had wanted to pick her up from Gatwick but Ali preferred to meet him in private; she wanted to look into his eyes and to know that she was doing the right thing. She realised more clearly than ever that Jack's affair had truly changed things between them. Normally, returning from trips away, she'd be full of excitement, longing to run inside and wrap her arms around her husband, breathing in his familiar smell, chattering away about her exploits and showing him what she'd bought. This time Ali felt nervous and slightly sick and saw that it was going to take her longer than she'd thought to recover from what had happened.

When she opened the front door and walked through into the kitchen, the first person she saw was not Jack but her daughter Lucy. Jack came over and, rather tentatively, gave Ali a hug. He looked searchingly into her eyes but Ali was preoccupied with the presence of her daughter. It was strange that she was at the cottage as her university term would be over in a few weeks and then Lucy would come home for the rest of the summer. Ali wondered if Jack had told Lucy about the affair but, in answer to Ali's questioning look, he gave her a bemused shrug and so she was relieved to see that was not the case.

"Lucy, what a wonderful surprise. Oh, it's so lovely to see you."

Ali went over and put her arms around her daughter but Lucy flinched and pulled away. Ali noticed for the first time how awful she looked. She was still in her dressing gown, her hair was lank and flat and there were dark circles under her eyes.

"I thought I'd come and see you both. That's OK isn't it? I thought you were coming back yesterday. In fact, I didn't know until I arrived last night that you'd gone away without Dad."

Lucy sounded resentful and sullen and Ali, fearing that her daughter had instinctively picked up on the tension between her parents, was anxious to reassure her. "It's the perfect homecoming, love. Now, have you eaten? I've had nothing all day except a soggy cheese sandwich on the plane that cost me about twenty quid. Let me have a quick shower and then shall we go to The Feathers for a late lunch?"

But Lucy said that she felt tired and she'd rather go back to bed. Ali and Jack stayed in the kitchen discussing their daughter; their own problems seemed trivial and childish in light of the fact that there was clearly something wrong with Lucy.

Ali had been twenty-five when she'd had Lucy. She wasn't a solicitor then but worked in the office of an insurance company. The job wasn't particularly exciting or well-paid and, rather than put Lucy in a nursery, they decided that Ali would give up work when Lucy was born, for the first few years at least. Jack had been recently promoted and, if they were careful and only ate on alternate days, they could just about manage on his salary.

Ali was surprised at how isolated and lonely she felt after Lucy's birth. None of her friends had children and, although she'd taken Lucy to the library and the park, none of the other mothers there seemed to be her type or even particularly friendly. She tried a local young mothers' group but stopped going because the woman who ran it insisted on calling everyone "Mummy" instead of by their names and no one appeared to be interested in talking about current affairs or even TV; their sole topic of conversation was babies.

Two things saved her; one was starting an evening class in A level law and the other was meeting Carolyn. Ali had noticed that the Salvation Army hall in the village displayed a poster advertising a mother and baby club, held every Wednesday afternoon. She went more from curiosity than anything else, half expecting they'd be made to march up and down, singing lustily; actually she rather hoped that would be the case.

Sitting on a chair with Lucy on a mat at her feet, Ali found that the meeting did indeed start with a prayer and, glancing to her left, she noticed one of the other mothers raising her eyebrows and mouthing "bloody hell". Ali started to laugh causing the uniformed Salvation Army person to pause and look at her sharply, which made the other mother laugh too. They both spent the entire prayer shaking with suppressed giggles. It was like being back at school; it was heavenly.

Carolyn introduced herself and they had been close friends ever since. She had a baby boy similar in age to Lucy and a three-year-old daughter who was delighted to have two babies to mother. On most days Ali would wave Jack off to work, quickly do whatever housework there was and then push Lucy round to Carolyn's house. It was so much easier and much more fun looking after babies when there were two of you. Ali could quite see why people joined communes. She'd have joined one herself but she had a feeling that they frowned on high heels and bacon sandwiches and she couldn't live without either.

Carolyn was attractive rather than pretty. Her features were a little sharp and she had a long chin which she disguised by wearing her dark straight hair in a geometric bob. She was tall and very slim; after giving birth to both of her children she'd fitted back into her jeans within days, which hadn't endeared her to the other mothers. As the only child of rich parents, she was self-assured and opinionated, saved from arrogance by an innate kindness.

It was to Carolyn that Ali had first revealed her plan to study law and become a solicitor. Fearing that Carolyn would be scornfully dismissive of her ambitions, Ali was touched by her friend's enthusiastic response and she started to believe that she might actually achieve her goal.

Lucy had always been sensitive. As a small child she'd cry piteously if they saw a dead bird or even a beetle. Books and films with sad endings had to be avoided and she became very upset if anyone shouted or even raised their voice. Ali hardly ever needed to tell her off; a look of disappointment was enough to produce a flood of remorse. Ali and Jack worried that they were to blame for their daughter's fragility; perhaps they had been too protective towards their only child. If there had been brothers or sisters maybe Lucy would have been more robust. They had wanted more children but it had just never happened.

During her school years Lucy always made friends with the most unusual child in her class. One girl was immensely tall; another lived with her grandparents and wore unfashionably long school skirts with stout lace-up shoes.

Jack and Ali were proud of their daughter's caring nature; it seemed inevitable that the children Lucy befriended would otherwise be shunned and probably bullied at school. They admired her for being an individual and, if they sometimes wished that Lucy would come home from school arm in arm with the netball captain, they kept it to themselves.

Given Lucy's choice of school friends, Jack used to joke with Ali about what her first boyfriend would be like. He thought a fruitarian who would live in a caravan and take Lucy scrumping. Ali favoured a mime artist in a travelling circus. They were pleasantly surprised then when a boy of about seventeen, Lucy's age, came to the cottage one day and asked for her. He had a friendly, open face and, when invited in, chatted to them politely. When Lucy came down, blushing furiously, he told her that she looked nice and then asked Jack if it was OK if he and Lucy went for a walk. When the pair had left, Jack and Ali gazed at each other.

"Well, he seemed pretty normal. Do you know, when he spoke to me he looked me straight in the eye. Not many kids today do that."

"Yes, but what I want to know is how are his circus skills." joked Ali. "Anyway, it looked like their first date.

Let's not get carried away. We'll probably never hear of him again."

But Lucy and the boy, Mason, dated for the rest of that year and became increasingly close. Jack and Ali liked him well enough. He had a pleasant manner, was very attentive to Lucy and polite to them. They didn't mind much that Mason had already left school and was working in a local garage. Lucy was in the sixth form and due to start university next year. Jack and Ali felt it was unlikely that the relationship would last once Lucy moved into a different world; one which brought her into contact with many other young men.

One evening, when Ali and Lucy were watching TV together, Lucy asked her mother if Jack had ever been jealous.

"Not really, Lucy. When we were first dating he did have a bit of a thing about my boss at the time. Your Dad seemed to think that I fancied him. It was quite funny actually because I didn't at all; he looked a bit like Burt Reynolds."

"Who?"

"Never mind. Why do you ask, love?"

"Oh, no reason. I just wondered."

Lucy never brought up the subject again but it had made Ali feel uneasy and she wasn't sure why.

Not long afterwards, Lucy came home from an evening with Mason in tears and told Ali that it was all over. She said that there was no reason in particular and Ali was relieved; not only because Lucy could now concentrate on her exams but because she had begun to dislike Mason for reasons she couldn't quite articulate.

For some weeks Lucy remained quiet and withdrawn, not going out much but staying in her room, studying. Ali tiptoed around her, cooking her favourite meals and buying her little gifts in an attempt to lighten her spirits. She was pleased to see that her efforts seemed to be working. Lucy became her old self again, going out to see friends and taking care over her appearance. The reason for this soon became clear when Lucy came down to breakfast one morning and announced, with shining eyes, that she and Mason were back together. Seeing their daughter so happy, Jack and Ali couldn't be sorry about this but they were both very glad that Lucy would be moving away soon.

Once the A level exams were over, Lucy and three of her friends were going to Cornwall for a week's holiday. They'd planned it for months, searching the net for the coolest restaurants and bars and making endless lists of the clothes they would need,

"Are you sure you will need five pairs of shoes, Lucy?" said Jack, peering over her shoulder to read the "MUST HAVE!" list on her laptop.

"You're probably right, Dad. I'll change it to six."

"Oh, make it seven, why don't you?" Jack grinned. "Your mother would."

The day before the girls were due to leave, Lucy told her parents that she'd changed her mind and she wasn't going.

"But why on earth not?" Ali said. She suddenly knew that Mason had something to do with it.

"It's Mason isn't it? He doesn't want you to go away without him. That's why you asked me about jealousy that time; he's jealous of you seeing your friends."

"Oh don't be so ridiculous, Mother. You don't know anything about it. You've never liked Mason just because he works in a garage. You're such a snob," and Lucy stormed out of the room.

Ali ran after her: "But you've been looking forward to this holiday for ages, Lucy. It's all paid for and, anyway, you can't let the other girls down."

I've nothing in common with them anymore. They're so silly and boring. I'm not going and that's that."

When Jack came home he tried to talk to Lucy but only ended up losing his temper. Nothing he or Ali could say would change Lucy's mind.

Ali and Jack finally had enough when Lucy said that she wasn't sure that she wanted to go to university. She'd got a place at Bath to study sociology. She'd done well to get in and they were both very proud of her. They sat her down and told her that they were not going to see her throw her life away over some boy. She could see him at weekends and in the holidays and Mason could go up to Bath and stay with her sometimes. Here Jack and Ali envisaged Mason being very out of place and comparing badly with Lucy's new university friends.

"You don't understand!" wailed Lucy. "We love each other."

"Well you won't stop loving one another just because you are 150 miles apart," said Ali, silently hoping they would do just that.

Eventually, after a long and tearful weekend (during which Mason was summoned and seemed oddly accepting of the situation), Lucy said she would take up her place in September after all.

CHAPTER NINE

It had been nine months ago and now Ali hoped that Mason was not the cause of Lucy's current distress. Throughout her first year at university she'd hardly mentioned him. Various other new friends were talked of, boys included, and Jack and Ali had congratulated themselves on dealing well with what they called "the Mason situation". Clearly, what they had expected had happened; Lucy had outgrown Mason and moved on. To think that he was still in her life and causing her pain was unbearable.

"Look," said Ali to Jack. "She seems exhausted. We'll leave her for today and I'll have a talk with her in the morning. It's Sunday tomorrow, why don't you go and have a game of golf; I think she may say more if it's just me and her."

Jack looked hurt and so Ali added, "You know how she looks up to you and wants you to be proud of her. If she's got herself into a mess, she may be reluctant to tell you about it" – Ali paused – "and I know that we need to talk about us but I can't think of anything but Lucy right now."

Once Jack had left the next morning, Ali made a mug of tea and took it up to Lucy's room. She knocked gently and then opened the door. Lucy was still asleep and, as she had often done as a child, had thrown the covers off the bed so that they lay in a heap on the floor. Putting the tea down, Ali went to the bed to pull the sheets over her daughter. Asleep, she looked so young; like a little girl. Ali was about to cover Lucy up when she stepped back in horror, raising her hand to her mouth and letting out a low moan. Both of Lucy's arms were covered in bruises and there were further bruises on her hip and thigh. They were all different colours; some were purple, almost black, whilst the ones on her thigh were yellow, tinged with green.

As Ali stood over her daughter, Lucy opened her eyes

and frantically scrambled for the sheets, trying to pull them over her body,

"What are you doing staring at me while I'm asleep? Get out, get out and leave me alone."

With her last few words Lucy's voice had risen into a scream. She tried to hide herself but the sheets had become entangled. Ali gently held both of her hands until the girl stopped struggling. Lucy began to cry silently, her tears falling onto her mother's hands.

Ali sat sideways on Lucy's bed, leaning against the wall, with Lucy's head in her lap. Whilst her mother gently and rhythmically stroked her hair, Lucy began to talk. "Mason's always been possessive. At first, I liked it; I thought it meant that he was really into me. He'd say that he didn't need anyone else apart from me in his life and, if I loved him, then I should feel the same.

"When I went to Bath, he moved there too. I didn't tell you and Dad because I knew you'd be angry. He found a job with a tyre place and got a room in this grotty house. At first, it was great. He tried hard to fit in, he'd come to parties with me and was really nice to my friends. But then he started questioning me; if we'd been out somewhere and met up with some uni friends, when we got home he'd accuse me of flirting with all the men. He'd go on and on about it. He'd turn up at the Union bar and say we'd have to leave; I'd come out of lectures to find him waiting for me.

"He thought I was sleeping with everyone, even my statistics lecturer who's about ninety-three. In the end, it was just easier to avoid other people; well, they soon avoided me once I started saying no to every invitation. I didn't even dare have a coffee with someone in case Mason showed up and caused a scene. He lost his job because he kept taking time off and he was drinking a lot and so, well, it just got worse."

Ali forced herself to keep quiet and not interrupt.

"One day, a couple of months ago, I ran into one of my

friends from halls and her boyfriend."

Lucy shifted on Ali's lap.

"I'd more or less moved out of my room and into Mason's place and I hadn't seen her for a while. Well, it was just so nice to see her and when she said that they were going for a drink and why didn't I join them, I thought why not? Why shouldn't I go for a drink on a Sunday afternoon like any normal student?

"I don't know how Mason knew I was there; he must have been following me, I guess. Anyway, he walked into the pub, sat down at our table and started chatting. The others didn't notice anything wrong, but I did. He was being too nice – you know. I tried to get him to leave but he kept saying that he was having fun and he drank quite a lot."

Lucy paused, glanced at Ali and then looked down again, her fingers compulsively twisting the cord on her dressing gown.

"When we got back to his room, he didn't say a word and I began to hope that maybe it would be OK but then he walked over to me" – Lucy started to sob – "and he punched me in the face."

Ali felt her body tense with fury but she forced herself to stay calm. "Go on, love, what happened next?"

"Oh, as soon as he'd done it he was distraught. He kept saying over and over again that he was sorry and he begged me not to tell anyone; not to tell you and Dad."

"But why didn't you, Luce? Why couldn't you come to us?"

"I was just so ashamed, Mum. And also I thought, well, maybe it was somehow my fault; if I'd behaved differently then Mason wouldn't have hit me. Anyway, for a while things got better, Mason was really sweet to me. Then, one day, I was walking through the uni grounds with Mason and my personal tutor came over. She'd asked me about a bruise on my eye a few weeks before (I hadn't mentioned that to Mason, of course). I'd told her some story about my walking into a cupboard but I don't think she believed me.

"This time she said, 'Is this your boyfriend?' and she started asking Mason all these questions, like *was he a student?* And *where did he live?* When we got back to his place, Mason went mad, shouting that I'd betrayed him and he punched me again, only this time on my body where the bruises wouldn't show. After that it happened all the time, anything could set him off; he even stopped apologising afterwards.

"When I got your text from Spain last week, I just really, really wanted to see you. On Friday I pretended that I was going to a lecture as usual and I got the train here. I hadn't planned to say anything; I just wanted to feel normal for a while."

Ali wrapped her arms around Lucy and rocked her to and fro. "You are safe now, I'm here. We'll wait until your Dad comes back and then we'll go to the police station. They will want to take some photographs. No one can hurt you any more, love. You'll never have to be alone with him again."

Lucy sat up and looked directly at her mother. "No, no police; I don't want that. Promise me that you won't go to the police."

"But, Lucy, what that man has done is a criminal offence. He needs to be locked up. You can't let him get away with it. None of this is your fault, you do know that?"

Lucy bit her lip: "The thing is, Mum, he's got some photos, photos of me; well, you know. He says that if I tell anyone what he's done then he'll put them on Facebook. I couldn't stand that, Mum. My life would be over."

CHAPTER TEN

Two hours later Ali and Lucy were driving towards Bath in Ali's little Honda. Lucy slept most of the way and Ali drove in silence, thinking about what she was going to say to Mason.

They'd decided not to tell Jack for the time being. He would need to know later but, if they told him now, he'd insist on calling the police or would rush off and confront Mason. Ali wanted to kill Mason herself but, if they were to get him out of their lives, it would need cool logical planning, not violence.

Lucy woke up as they were approaching the city centre and directed Ali to a dreary looking street lined with tall, dilapidated terraced houses. Number 16 had been divided into flats. At the side of the front door were a number of buzzers, some with handwritten names alongside.

Ali had Lucy's keys and, while her daughter waited in the car, she opened the front door and stepped into a narrow hallway, its dirty tiled floor strewn with fliers and unclaimed post. Ali made her way upstairs to flat 2C and, taking a deep breath, turned the key in the flimsy door.

The flat was really just one room. Ali took in a double bed under a window, a sagging sofa facing an enormous TV and, standing in a kitchen alcove, Mason. He glanced beyond her before saying, "Oh, it's you. What do you want? Where's Lucy? Is she with you?"

Mason's manner was aggressive but Ali could see from his eyes that he was scared. *He is so young*, she thought, the same age as Lucy; just a boy really. She saw now that his dark, handsome face had a weakness to it and thought with some satisfaction that it wouldn't be too long before he'd lose his good looks and would no longer be able to manipulate innocent girls.

Ali sat calmly on the sofa, pushing to one side several car magazines and an empty beer bottle and started her rehearsed speech. She blanked the images of Lucy's bruised body from her mind and imagined that she was presenting a case on behalf of a client.

"Lucy is not here. She is at home with her father. Lucy has told her father and me everything that you have done to her and, indeed, we have seen the injuries for ourselves. They have, of course, been photographically recorded."

Mason tried to interrupt but Ali held up her hand and said, "I am speaking now." She continued: "I think you are aware that I am a lawyer. As you would expect I have close ties, very close ties, with the criminal courts and am personal friends with several judges. One of them, in particular, owes me a favour and I am about to call it in."

Ali glanced at Mason, wondering if she'd gone too far. As a commercial property solicitor, she never went near a court (and hadn't since she'd been a trainee), but she figured that Mason's knowledge of the legal system would be based solely on American TV crime dramas.

"I don't know if Lucy has told you Mason (how she hated saying her daughter's name in this ghastly room) but her Godfather is the Chief of Police in this very area. One phone call to him will have you locked up so fast that your head will spin; and his coppers are loyal – very loyal, if you see what I mean."

Lucy's Godfather, a mild, bespectacled librarian, would be very surprised to hear this.

Mason's shoulders started to slump and it looked as though he was about to cry and Ali thought it was the right time to back off a little.

"Now, Lucy is a very sweet girl, as well you know and, for some reason, she wants to give you a chance. If you promise me that you will move away from here and never contact Lucy again then I will consider not involving the police."

Hope seeped into Mason's eyes and, with it, some of his previous bravado, "Yeah, well, I can't go yet. I've just paid the rent on this place and I'd need to pay in advance for a new flat."

Ali couldn't believe that this little shit could actually

think that she'd give him money when she realised this was turning out better than she'd hoped, "How much are we talking about? I need to know that you will leave tonight. Would £500 cover it?"

" A thousand would be better; cash though; I'm not taking a cheque."

"I can do better than that; I'll transfer £1,000 into your account right now." Ali got out her phone. "What's your account number?"

Ali thought that Mason may refuse and insist on cash but greed took over and minutes later she had a record of the internet bank transfer into Mason's account on her phone and could show Lucy, in case she had any lingering feelings for him, just how highly he valued her love. It seemed harsh but Ali was well aware of her daughter's kind heart and she had to make sure that Lucy would never go back to him.

"Just one more thing. I understand that you have threatened to publish some photographs of Lucy. If they ever appear, anywhere at any time in the next 100 years, I will make those calls to the Chief Inspector and to the judge. If those photos are made public, you will be classified as a sex offender and you know how they treat sex offenders in prison, don't you, Mason? If I were you, I'd destroy the photos now, in case they accidently get out there."

Again, Ali was skirting the truth but, as Mason seemed to believe her, she went further, "The same applies if either I, Lucy or my husband see you again or if I find out that you have assaulted any other girls. Through my contacts, I can register your face on the FRC, that's the police Face Recognition Computer. If you so much as steal a packet of crisps, I'll come after you; are we clear?

"Now, I'll just take Lucy's laptop. I'm not bothered about her clothes and other things."

Ali wanted Lucy to have as few reminders as possible of her time in this room.

Holding the laptop under her arm, Ali walked over to

Mason. Up close his eyes looked puffy and bloodshot. She glanced down at his hands, the fingers stained with oil and thought of what they had done to Lucy. Raising her free arm she slapped him with as much force as she could across his face. Although Mason clenched his fists, he didn't retaliate and Ali quickly turned and left the room.

Driving back home on her own that evening, Ali wondered if she'd done the right thing in not going straight to the police. She felt confident that Mason would stay away from Lucy but Ali knew that it wouldn't be long before he found another girl to bully. Her priority, however, had to be her own daughter and Ali had to respect Lucy's wish not to report Mason; it was Lucy's life and Lucy's decision.

Ali had told her daughter about the conversation with Mason, including the fact that he'd accepted money to move away and that she'd slapped his face before she left. She'd looked at Lucy, dreading to see hurt in her face but, to her relief, Lucy had smiled and said, "You hit him? Oh, Mum, I'd wish I'd seen that."

She had driven Lucy to her halls. Her roommates seemed surprised to see her but, when Ali left, they were all busy cooking pasta and Lucy, looking a little pale, had waved Ali off happily enough. Ali drove away, feeling a little as she had when she'd left Lucy at nursery school for the first time.

When Ali got home Jack was waiting up for her. She'd decided on the journey back that she wouldn't tell him the full story just yet; she'd let things settle down first. She told him that Lucy had become stressed about the end of year exams but that she'd managed to calm her down and that Lucy had seemed fine when she left her. All of that was true; it just wasn't the whole truth.

Ali suggested to Jack that they meet after work the next evening at Harvey's, a Bistro in town and have a long overdue discussion of their own situation. She added that she was tired after her drive and that she would sleep in the spare room that night. She wasn't ready to jump into his arms quite yet.

CHAPTER ELEVEN

The next day Ali was at her desk by eight o'clock. She'd been away for a week but it felt much longer. Most of her morning was spent catching up on emails. Liz, the secretary she shared with another partner had dealt with some of them but Ali still had hundreds more to respond to.

At lunchtime there was a buffet in the boardroom for the trainees who were due to start at Cassell Brookes and Little in September. As usual, they were polite and nervous. Ali looked forward to seeing their personalities emerge once they started work and relaxed into their roles. The firm had taken on just two trainees this year; a sign of the downturn in the economy which had affected Ali's property department in particular and had also slowed down the corporate deals. Divorce and Litigation, in contrast, tended to thrive in a recession.

As she always did, Ali asked the trainees, a male and a female, both with first class degrees from good universities, what they thought was the main purpose of the firm. Trainees invariably said that it was to help clients solve their legal problems; some went so far as to say that the role of the firm was to right injustices in society. The male trainee spoke at some length along these predictable lines, turning quite pink as he warmed to his theme. Ali was pleased when the woman answered that the main function of the firm was to make money for the partners and made a mental note to ensure that the trainee spent at least one of her six-month placements in Ali's own department.

By seven o'clock, Ali was sitting at a table for two in Harvey's. Jack had called to say that he might be a few minutes late and Ali welcomed the time to collect her thoughts. She had been so preoccupied with Lucy that she'd hardly thought about her and Jack or, indeed, Jack and Sarah Hill. Now, Ali found that the conclusions she had come to in Spain still held true. She loved Jack, thought she could forgive him and wanted their marriage to continue.

When Jack had arrived and they'd ordered drinks and their meal, Ali told him how she felt. His relief was immediate and obvious. Reaching across the table for her hand he said, "You have no idea how happy that makes me. I know that we can work this out. I'm going to spend the rest of my life making it up to you."

"I need to know, Jack, that you have never done anything like this before and that it will never happen again. I mean, I thought our life together was pretty perfect but there must have been something wrong to make you do this."

"Our life together is perfect, Ali. I've just been such a fool. I suppose it was my age or something. She made it very clear that she was attracted to me and I was stupid enough to feel flattered. Seeing the hurt on your face and knowing that I might have lost you, well, I can promise you, darling, that I have never even thought of being unfaithful before and I will never, ever do anything like this again.

"Do you want to know anything? You know, any details?"

A voice inside Ali's head was screaming, *Yes, Jack, I want to know what she was like in bed. Was she better than me?* But she answered: "No, I would like it very much if we never mentioned that woman again."

Jack nodded and turned his attention to his fillet steak.

"Although you have hurt me very deeply, Jack," he put his knife and fork down and reached for her hand again, "and it may take a long time for me to fully get over this..."

Jack waited to see if Ali would continue and, when she did not, he tentatively started eating again.

They talked of other matters. Ali told Jack about her week in Spain (omitting the incident with the nasty man in the bar) and they both discussed their work. Ali steered the conversation away from Lucy; she didn't want to have to tell any more lies.

Ali waved to the waiter for another glass of wine. Jack, who'd only had a small beer, switched to water and suggested that they leave Ali's car in town and he would bring her to work the next day.

A while later they drove home in silence. The tension between them made obvious by Ali's hunched shoulders and Jack's grim expression. They'd enjoyed their meal and Ali had even had a pudding, chocolate cheesecake accompanied, on the waiter's advice, by a large glass of Cointreau. Ali had a second glass whilst Jack drank his coffee and she suddenly found that she did want to talk about Sarah Hill; she wanted to very much indeed.

"You never brought her to our house, did you?" Ali asked, slightly too loudly. "I mean, I couldn't bear it if I knew she'd been in our bed. We'd have to buy a new one; in fact, we'd have to move house."

When Jack started to speak, Ali interrupted him, "What did you say about me? You must have discussed me with her. What did you tell her, Jack?"

By now Ali was more or less shouting and other diners were beginning to look around to their table.

"Ali, be quiet, people are staring," Jack hissed.

"Don't you tell me to be quiet. How dare you tell me what to do. I'll do what I bloody well like," and with that Ali poured the remains of her Cointreau over Jack's head and burst into tears.

The waiters fussed round and Jack bundled Ali out of the restaurant, signalling to the head waiter that he'd come and pay the next day.

Over breakfast the next morning, Ali told Jack that, whilst she was sorry to have caused a scene in Harvey's, she had every right to feel angry and she expected that she may behave very badly indeed over the coming months and he'd better get used to the idea. Jack, who'd clearly been hoping for a little more contrition, possibly even a slight balancing in the scale of marital misbehaviour, quietly accepted this; although he'd make sure they didn't buy any damned Cointreau in the future.

They parted outside Ali's office affectionately enough, although each were secretly relieved that Jack would be away with his work until Friday. Ali hoped that Jack would dwell on her emotional outburst and realise that it would take a lot of time and effort on his part before they were back to normal. Jack just hoped that Ali would have calmed down by the end of the week.

CHAPTER TWELVE

Ali's week went well. Free from distractions, she worked late into the evenings at the office, went to the gym and spoke on the phone to her sister Linda and to her daughter. To her sister she confided the whole truth about Lucy and was relieved that Linda agreed with what she had done,

"Lucy needed to take control of the situation, Ali. If you had gone to the police against Lucy's wishes then you would have disempowered her."

In the local council offices where Linda worked, disempowerment was spoken of with astonishing regularity, even in the most banal of conversations.

Linda was keen to know how Ali's solo holiday had gone and how things were now between Ali and Jack. She laughed a lot when she heard about the scene in the restaurant and thought to herself that she'd take a large bottle of Cointreau with her when she next visited.

Lucy seemed to be fine. She told Ali that the girls in her halls were being very supportive and, with her exams only days away, she'd hardly thought of Mason at all.

"I think when someone treats you so badly then you just stop loving them in the end."

On Thursday a letter arrived with the morning post and Ali recognised Jack's handwriting. It was a thing of his to send her handwritten letters. He'd done it since they first started dating and had continued to do so in an increasingly computerised age. The letter was quite short:

Wednesday   A faceless hotel somewhere in the Midlands

My Darling wife,

You must allow me to tell you how ardently I admire and love you. I have reserved a suite at Luckingham Hall for Friday and Saturday night. I will be waiting for you in the cocktail lounge at 6pm on Friday. I will be the one with his heart on his sleeve.

Your adoring husband,

Jack xxx

Ali realised that this was very clever of Jack. They hadn't slept together since she knew of his affair. In their own home, in their own bedroom, the first post affair occasion may be awkward, too significant somehow. In a king-size bed in a luxury hotel suite, sex would be the most natural thing in the world.

She briefly allowed the thought that Jack and Sarah had no doubt met in hotel rooms to enter her head but pushed it away. Luckingham Hall wasn't a hotel it was a "destination experience" according to the brochure Jack had included with his letter. Ali read through a list of spa treatments; this was going to be a lot of fun.

That evening Ali packed for the weekend. She would drive straight to the hotel after work the next day. She considered her wardrobe; definitely not the turquoise dress – too many bad memories of Carolyn's dinner party. She'd take her favourite black one; demur from the front but with a low, scooped back which would show off her tan.

Jack loved it when her shoulder length auburn hair was sleek and smooth and she decided to have a blow dry at lunchtime, if the salon could fit her in. Ali thought about buying some new silky underwear but decided that she didn't want Jack to think that she was trying too hard; that was his job. In the old, pre-affair days, she'd have packed her old high necked nightie that Jack's mother had given to her one Christmas and worn it primly to bed to make Jack laugh. This time she was going to make damn sure that she looked very sexy indeed.

At the office on Friday morning, Ali told her secretary Liz that she'd be leaving early that day, at about half past four. Liz walked over to Ali's desk.

"A new client called to make an appointment last week, a Mrs Keeling. I've put her in at four o'clock. Shall I rearrange it?"

"Do you know what it's about?"

"No, only that she asked for you specifically. I offered to make her an appointment with one of the other solicitors, as you were on holiday, but she said that she preferred to wait and see you. She said that she wouldn't need much of your time; hopefully half an hour will do it."

Ali doubted that very much. The first meeting with a new client invariably took ages. Merely explaining to them what identification they needed to supply before a file could be opened took about twenty minutes. The Law Society had become paranoid about money being laundered through property deals. Well, she was determined not to be delayed. She'd just get the basic facts and then make another appointment for next week. It was probably a dispute with a neighbour over a boundary line being moved four inches; people had been known to shoot one another over less.

On being told that Mrs Keeling had arrived and been installed in one of the ground floor meeting rooms, Ali turned off her PC and told Liz that she'd leave straight after seeing the client, rather than come back up to her office where she'd be bound to be waylaid over something or other.

Mrs Keeling jumped nervously when Ali walked into the meeting room. She was a small, birdlike woman in her fifties with badly dyed reddish hair and, although dressed smartly in a white blouse and navy skirt, she looked nothing like Ali's usual clients.

Ali introduced herself and, forgoing the offer of tea or coffee to save time, she smiled and said, "How can I help you, Mrs Keeling?"

The woman fiddled with her scarf and cleared her throat. Ali leaned forward encouragingly. "You know that I specialise in commercial property matters? Are you thinking of opening a new night club?"

Neither of the women laughed and Ali felt a prick of unease. Mrs Keeling was looking at her not with apprehension or deference but with what appeared to be pity. All of a sudden she began to talk, "The thing is, there is something you should know." She cleared her throat again before continuing:

"I clean for Mrs Hill up at the old tannery site."

For a moment Ali couldn't think who she meant. Mrs Hill? Of course, Sarah Hill. My God, Ali thought, *has this woman come here in her cheap blouse to tell me of Jack's affair?* How dare she! Ali felt her face flush with anger.

Mrs Keeling was talking again, "You get to see things as a cleaner, you notice things like. You hear things too. She's always on the phone, Mrs Hill. Anyway, I thought to myself, she's playing away that one and then, one day, it was a Tuesday, my day for doing the windows, he came to the house. I knew straight away it was him, the way she kept simpering at him and touching his arm. And, of course, he's done it before you see, with our Katy."

Mrs Keeling paused and looked sadly at Ali. "I thought, no, you're not going to get away with it again and that's why I had to come and see you. To tell you about your husband."

Ali had hardly been taking in what Mrs Keeling was saying; she was so incensed at the woman coming in to her office and daring to tell her sordid tale. She'd risen from her seat to ask Mrs Keeling to leave when she finally registered the woman's deadly words.

Sitting back down, Ali tried to make her voice sound normal: "Katy?" Her hands had started to shake and she pushed them under the table.

"I'm sorry to be telling you all this, Mrs Jones. I really am. Katy is my daughter. She's a lovely girl but a bit stupid where men are concerned. She's twenty-nine but she's been living back with me and my husband since her divorce, two years ago now it must be.

"Anyway, John and I never minded her going out and about, she's still young after all. About twelve months ago, she started mentioning this chap, it was Jack this and Jack that."

Ali sat, her eyes fixed on the other woman's face. Her whole body had begun to tremble as though she was icy cold. Mrs Keeling looked at Ali defiantly.

"She never knew he was married. Oh no, he kept that from her. It went on for months. We thought it was strange that he never came into the house. He'd just pull up outside in that big car of his and she'd go running out. I'd watch him from the window; he always got out, see, and opened the car door for her – a real gent."

Mrs Keeling pursed her lips and went on, "When she found out that he had a wife, it broke her heart. She saw a picture of you and him in the local paper, at some charity do in town. Mr and Mrs Jack Jones it said. She never saw him again. I don't know if she spoke to him to tell him that she knew or not. I don't suppose my husband and I would have found out about him being married if she hadn't taken them pills."

Ali put her hand to her mouth, "Did she, I mean, is she all right?"

"The doctor said that she hadn't taken enough to do any real harm but they kept her in for a few days to be on the safe side. I found the newspaper with the photo in her bedroom when I went to get her nightie for the hospital. The article said that you worked here and I recognised him straight off.

"I was all for coming to see you then but Mr Keeling said best to leave well alone. When I found out that he was at it again I said, 'Well, I'm going to let that poor woman know what sort of man she's married to.' I chucked that newspaper in the bin, along with some letters she'd kept in a drawer. Handwritten they were, on fancy paper. They went in the bin too."

Ali was alone in the meeting room. She glanced at her watch – 6.30pm – she'd been sitting in the room for two hours after Mrs Keeling had left. She didn't remember her leaving; presumably after delivering her devastating message she'd just got up and walked out.

She heard voices in the corridor, "Jonesy must have finished her meeting by now. Let's see if she wants to go for a pint."

Ali just had time to turn her back to the door and put her phone to her ear before the door opened and two of her colleagues peered in. Mike Peterson and John Greenway, her Friday night drinking buddies.

"Ali, we're off to The Vaults. Are you coming?"

Not trusting herself to speak and not wanting them to see her tear-stained face, she kept her back to them and waved her phone in the air, so that they could see she was occupied. Thankfully they left, muttering that she'd do anything to avoid buying the first round. She heard Mike say, "I bet she's not even on the phone at all," and their laughter tailed off as they left the building.

Ali thought of Jack who'd be sitting in the hotel bar by now, wondering where she was. She made three phone calls in quick succession and then switched her phone off.

First, she phoned Luckingham Hall and asked them to give a message to Mr Jack Jones. "Tell him," she said, "that Katy isn't coming."

Then she called a taxi firm and ordered a cab to the station. She was in no state to drive.

Finally, she called her friend Emma and asked if she could come and stay. "Jack and I are finished," she said and then rang off.

Emma put the phone down and sighed. She'd been expecting that call for a long, long time.

CHAPTER THIRTEEN

When Emma was twenty-two she met the man she would love for the rest of her life. He was a friend of her flat mate and when he walked into their local pub one cold winter evening and Emma's friend said casually, "Oh, everyone, this is Simon."

Emma knew with absolute certainty that this was the man she was going to marry.

He wasn't conventionally handsome, his eyes were too deep-set and his nose too large but he had a beautiful humorous mouth and a way of looking directly at the person he was talking to, as though they were the most fascinating person in the world.

Simon had called Emma the day after they met and soon they were seeing one another nearly every evening. Emma had never been happier and, when they had been together for ten months and Simon said one night that he had something to tell her, she assumed that he was going to propose. Instead, he looked deeply into her eyes and said that, although he was very fond of her, he wasn't sure that their relationship was going anywhere and maybe they should take a break for a while.

Emma's happy smile of anticipation had frozen on her lips and Simon, relieved that she appeared to be taking it quite well, hurried on, "We can still be friends though, Ems, can't we?"

And, for more than twenty years, they had been just that. They spent birthdays and Christmases together, celebrated one another's triumphs and commiserated woes. Very close friends indeed; the only problem was that one of them was still hopelessly in love and the other didn't know it.

Emma's other friends, Ali included, tried to persuade Emma to see less of Simon; they told her that she'd never meet anyone else if she kept comparing them to him. Simon had never married or settled down with another woman. He'd had a string of girlfriends, all of whom he'd introduce to Emma. None of them lasted very long and Emma would be summoned to accompany him to the opening of a new restaurant or gallery until another new girlfriend came along.

Ali had a theory that the reason Simon had never married was that he was secretly in love with Emma. "Imagine that, Em, both of you in love and neither of you aware of it. Why don't you tell him how you really feel? What have you got to lose?"

"Him, Ali. I could lose him. Don't you see? I can manage as we are, we see each other all the time. If I scare him away with some declaration of love and I never see him again, I don't think I could survive that."

Ali couldn't help blaming Simon for what she saw as ruining her friend's life. He could be very charming when it suited him but, right from the start, she'd found him self-centred and, if things weren't going his way, moody. When she saw him deep in conversation with someone, focusing on them with his intense gaze, she knew that the subject matter was more than likely to be Simon himself. That Emma, who knew him so well and who was so clever, couldn't see this was a mystery to Ali.

Emma had a very well paid and stressful job in the foreign currencies department of a private bank. She'd left school at the same time as Ali with a handful of O' levels and joined the local branch of a high street bank as a cashier. When an opportunity arose to move to the main London office, she took it. Sharing a flat in the wrong part of Islington, she became adept at the rush hour commute, powering along pavements in her trainers with her office heels in her bag.

Lacking a degree, it had taken Emma a long time to rise in her career but she was bright and determined, worked extremely hard and, eventually, she reached her current position which had enabled her to buy a small terraced cottage facing a green in West London, which she filled with John Lewis furniture and two ginger cats.

In addition to her lack of a university education, Emma had found it difficult to advance at work because she didn't look like a currencies trader. She was small and slim with very straight long blonde hair and neat, even features. Even in her forties she looked, from a distance, like a young girl. As a child she'd been extremely pretty but, as she'd grown, she'd become rather ordinary looking, apart from her hair, which she had expertly coloured and cut every six weeks.

Although Emma looked childlike and demur, in character she was adventurous and brave. She loved to take holidays in remote places, usually involving some kind of physical challenge; white water rafting in New Zealand or horse riding in the Serengeti. Whenever she and Ali went on a city break, Emma would explore whilst Ali had a siesta, coming back to their hotel to say that she'd found an amazing restaurant or met a local man who could take them on a tour of some underground vaults. Ali would cautiously venture out, her purse tucked firmly inside her bra, expecting to be ambushed at any moment, whilst her friend danced ahead, chattering to everyone they met in what she fondly imagined was the local dialect.

Ali had been unable to face the train journey to West London, which would involve going into the centre of the city and then out again, and had asked the taxi driver to take her the whole way. The cost had been horrendous but at least she didn't have to speak to anyone. She closed her eyes to discourage the driver from talking and tried not to think about anything at all except arriving at Emma's door. She realised when they'd been driving for about an hour that she'd left her case in her car at the office. Emma always had plenty of luxurious toiletries in the en suite of her spare room but Ali could hardly wear her friend's doll sized clothes. Normally, such a thought would have made Ali smile but, right now, she couldn't imagine ever smiling again.

Everything that she knew and had relied upon had

gone. The confident and optimistic woman had been replaced by a pathetic creature shrouded in dread and despair. She supposed, in time, that the depth of her misery might lessen but she could see no joy in her future years.

It was nearly nine o'clock before the taxi approached the green and pulled up outside Emma's smart cottage. Emma opened the front door before Ali had rung the bell and, bustling her inside, reached up to give her friend a long hug.

"Now, I know you won't have eaten and you don't think you want anything so I've just got us some lovely yummy things to pick at. But first you're going to need this."

Emma sat Ali down in the sleek kitchen at the back of the cottage and handed her a large glass of white wine.

"Would you like to have a bath whilst I put the food out? Or shall we talk first?"

Ali wasn't sure that she had the energy to move but her office clothes felt tight and uncomfortable.

"Can I just change out of these things for now? Have you got a dressing gown or something I can put on? I haven't got anything with me."

Ali started to cry and Emma gently led her upstairs to the pretty yellow and white spare bedroom.

"Take your time. Shout if you need anything. I've put some Jo Malone shower gel in there." Emma pointed to the bathroom: "And there's one of Simon's old dressing gowns on your bed."

Her friend's kindness made Ali cry again but, after a shower, she felt a little better and, with her hair in a turban and smelling deliciously of mandarin and grapefruit, she put on Simon's robe and went downstairs.

Emma's cottage had originally been a two up, two down but it had been extended so that, on the ground floor, there was a small square sitting room with a lovely original fireplace and, to the rear, a large kitchen diner with French doors opening onto a walled garden. Upstairs, on the first floor, was Emma's bedroom, bathroom and study and, in what had been the loft, a spare bedroom with an en suite bathroom.

Emma wasn't particularly interested in interior design but luckily the whole house had been totally remodelled and tastefully decorated when she'd bought it. She'd acquired many of the fittings with the house and several trips to John Lewis had supplied the rest.

The friends sat opposite one another at the French pine table, now arrayed with bowls of prawn mayonnaise, smoked salmon and cherry tomatoes and Emma said, "OK, sweetie, do you want to tell me what this is all about?"

Ali topped up her glass from a bottle on the table and took a deep breath, "I suppose I'd better start at the beginning."

She told Emma about Carolyn's birthday party and what she'd seen in the photographs. She went on to describe the dinner party and the row she'd had with Jack when they got home. She told her about Jack's confession of his affair with Sarah Hill, which had led to Ali's solitary week in Spain. With bitterness in her voice Ali recounted how, on her return, she'd wanted to forgive Jack and had believed his passionate assurances that the affair had been a one off.

Ali paused, distractedly picking up and then putting down a tomato without eating it. Emma poured herself another Vodka and tonic and encouraged her friend to continue: "Go on, Ali, what happened next?"

Ali then told Emma of the meeting with Mrs Keeling. She found that she could remember it word for word: "He'd even sent letters to this Katy; like he did to me, remember? I feel as though my whole marriage has been a lie, Emma. I mean, there was Sarah Hill and Katy; how many other women have there been? Has he been unfaithful throughout our whole marriage?

"How did I not know? Why didn't I notice any signs? To think that he must have left those women and then climbed straight into bed with me. What sort of a monster am I married to?"

Emma got up and put her arm around Ali. "I thought I'd never tell you about this, Ali, but something happened once between me and Jack."

Ali sat back and stared at her friend, "Not you as well, Emma? Not with Jack? Please don't tell me that."

Ali jumped up and paced over to the window.

"Of course I've never slept with him. I'd never do that, Ali, you know that." She paused. "But he did try it on with me once. In fact, he came on very strongly. I thought at one point that he was going to force himself on me.

"It was just after Lucy was born. I'd come up to see you and I was going to stay for a few days. I was so excited that you'd had a daughter. Well, you were very tired, obviously, and you'd gone up to bed. Jack and I stayed downstairs having a drink.

"Jack came and sat next to me on the sofa. I gave him a hug; I was so thrilled for him. We'd both had quite a bit to drink but I realised that he was very drunk, he was slurring his words. He put his arm around me and, at first, it seemed normal, like two old friends. But then he leant forward and tried to kiss me on the lips. I turned my head but he kept saying, 'Come on, Emma, give Daddy a kiss.' It was awful. I tried to push him away but he was so strong.

"He somehow pushed me down onto the sofa so that I was on my back and he lay on top of me. I didn't want to scream in case you heard but I kept hitting him with my fists and trying to get free. Then he started pulling at my clothes, he ripped my shirt; I thought he was going to rape me, Ali.

"Then Lucy started to cry and I heard you moving about upstairs. He jumped up then and went into the kitchen. I picked up my bag and ran out of the house. I just got in my car and drove home. I cried all the way, I couldn't believe what had happened.

"I'm sure you must have wondered why I'd left so suddenly. I've made sure that I've never been alone with him since."

Emma had persuaded Ali to get into bed, saying that she'd sit with her and talk for as long as she wanted. Emma hoped that, once Ali lay down, she'd fall asleep and she did do so, quite quickly. However, when Emma got up the next morning, she found Ali already awake and sitting in the garden drinking coffee.

"Did you manage to sleep for long?" Emma asked.

"Not really. I tried to read for a bit but I couldn't concentrate and so, about three, I came downstairs and watched a film. Don't ask me what it was about," Ali smiled wanly.

Emma managed to find Ali some clothes that sort of fitted; an old pair of jogging pants and a sweat shirt with a cat on the front and they spent the day talking and watching TV.

"Why did you never tell me about what happened with Jack?" asked Ali at one point.

"Oh, you were so happy, Ali, and Lucy was so tiny. How would you have coped on your own? So I decided not to say anything but I didn't realise how hard it would be to be around Jack, so I stayed away most of the time."

"I thought I'd lost you, Emma. I thought I'd lost my best friend."

"It was the same for me, Ali, but I thought that I was doing the right thing. I thought it was better for you to have Jack."

"I'm not sure that I ever did really have him, did I?" said Ali bitterly.

In the afternoon Emma got out some old photographs of the two of them at school and even Ali found herself laughing at their clothes and hairstyles.

"Oh look, here's one of us going to the school disco, Em. Do you remember your Mum said that if you wore your long black socks with your school shoes they'd look like skinny boots?"

"Yes, and everyone nearly died laughing when I

walked into the hall."

Emma had listened whilst Ali retold her story again and again; letting her talk and not making too many comments. One thing Emma did say to her friend was, "I think he does really love you, Ali, in his own way. He just doesn't know how to be faithful. You know how he loves to do adventurous things; maybe it's the excitement of it all."

"Well, you're the biggest adrenalin junky of all, Em, and you've loved the same man all your life."

"Yes, but what a man. I certainly pick them. You know, I heard him the other night saying to some woman, 'Let's talk about you. You seem to be a very perceptive person. What did you think when you saw me for the first time?'" Emma mimicked Simon's voice perfectly.

"Oh, he didn't, Emma," said Ali laughing. This was the first time that she'd really heard Emma say anything negative about Simon.

"I know what he's like, Ali. I realise that he's self-centred and vain. I just can't seem to stop loving him. In fact, it makes me love him all the more," she sighed. "I know, let's give up men for good and go and live on a Greek island together."

"Yes," said Ali. "We can weave our own caftans and ride around on donkeys. If we run out of money I can sleep with the tourists."

It was a running joke between them that, whenever they went away together, Ali would be propositioned. Men would sidle up to her and ask, "Are you working?" Sometimes Ali would see the same men in their hotel dining room with their wives and surreptitiously wink at them.

They had an early night and on Sunday morning Emma had some work to do so Ali went for a long walk. When she got back her thoughts were not much clearer but she did know that she didn't want to see Jack, not yet anyway. She'd turned her phone on a couple of times; there were several missed calls and four text messages, all from Jack, which she deleted without reading.

When Emma came down from her study, Ali asked her if it would be OK if she stayed for the rest of the week. "I just don't want to go back to the house. I can drive to the office from here if I avoid the rush hour and I can probably bring work from here on a couple of days."

Emma assured her that she could stay as long as she wanted. She offered to drive Ali home; she needed to collect some clothes and her car was still outside her office but Ali said that she'd take a taxi back on Monday morning; she'd go to work and then pick up what she needed from her house. Wanting to make sure that Jack wouldn't be there, Ali sent him a text:

'As you will have realised, I now know about Katy, and Emma has told me what you did to her. I am staying elsewhere for now. I don't want to see you or to speak to you. I'm coming to the house tomorrow to collect some things; don't be there. Do not say anything to Lucy. I will speak to her myself once her exams are over.'

She considered telling him that he'd broken her heart or calling him a bastard but thought that the flat, unemotional words would hurt him more. That was how she felt inside anyway; emotionally dead, as though she had used up all of her feelings and had none left.

Before turning her phone off, Ali sent a text to Lucy wishing her good luck with her exams, which started tomorrow. She wasn't sure yet how or when she could even begin to explain what had happened to her daughter. The thought of causing Lucy pain was unbearable and she worried how this would affect her daughter's already damaged view of men.

CHAPTER FOURTEEN

It was no good. Even if she lay flat on the bed, Ali's sister Linda couldn't zip up her jeans. Pulling on some forgiving leggings, she thought how unfair it was. She'd been really careful with her diet all week and had been to yoga and Pilates but she seemed to be fatter than ever; even her boobs looked bigger, for God's sake. Well Carl wouldn't complain about that. Not that he ever mentioned her weight; he always said she looked lovely even when she knew that she didn't.

Right, she'd cut down even further, stop drinking and live on rice cakes and water. She went downstairs to find her old fitness CD. It had to be here somewhere.

"Mrs Keeling, when you do the ironing, would you be an angel and press this," said Sarah Hill, holding up a cream silk blouse. "Mr Hill's taking me to Mason Pierre tonight, that new French restaurant in town. I don't know how he managed to get a table; it's been booked solid for weeks."

Mrs Keeling watched her employer's straight back leaving the room and was glad, on reflection, that she hadn't gone to Mr Hill with the news of his wife's infidelity. Mrs Hill did seem to be trying to make their marriage work and, anyway, she couldn't afford to lose her job. Indeed, her employer had been unusually nice to her recently; she'd asked if she wanted some clothes that she no longer wore and she'd given her a small rise. *I wonder*, thought Mrs Keeling, as she set up the ironing board, *if she suspects that I know what she's been up to*.

Turning on the radio, she started humming tunelessly; things had turned out quite well, all considered and she'd made sure that Jack Jones got what was coming to him. His wife looked quite ill when she left her; she wouldn't want to be in his shoes when he got home.

This silk blouse would look lovely with her navy skirt. Maybe, if she just accidentally scorched the sleeve, just a little, Mrs Hill would give it to her.

Luckily it was a fairly quiet time in Ali's office. She forced herself to concentrate on what work she had but often found that an hour had passed whilst she'd been staring at the same paragraph on her computer screen. Her secretary Liz clearly knew that something was amiss and fussed round her, digging for clues,

"Mr Jones alright, is he?" or "I expect Lucy will be glad to finish her exams this Friday."

Ali had spoken to Lucy in the week and agreed that she'd get the train to Emma's on Saturday morning and they'd spend the weekend there. Ali let Lucy assume that she would be driving to Emma's from home. It wasn't unusual for the three of them to spend the weekend together at Emma's cottage. Lucy loved the pubs by the Thames and Ali promised her that they'd go shopping to celebrate the end of her first year at university.

She'd felt a little guilty saying this, as she wasn't sure that either of them would feel like shopping once she'd told Lucy about her father. Ali still hadn't worked out exactly what she was going to say. She wanted to give her daughter enough information about what had happened so that Lucy would understand why her parent's marriage was over, without destroying her daughter's love and respect for her father. She wanted Jack to suffer but she also wanted Lucy to have a good relationship with him.

She and Emma had agreed that it would be best if she didn't tell Lucy about what had happened between Emma and Jack. In many ways, Jack's treatment of Emma had hurt Ali the most. How could he have been so arrogant to think that her best friend would sleep with him and worse, to try and force himself upon her. It had also meant that Emma had stayed away in those early years after Lucy's birth when Ali had desperately needed her.

Ali's client John Drake had called earlier in the week and asked if she was free for lunch on Friday. She readily agreed, thinking that his brash good humour was exactly what was needed right now and, as he no doubt had a new development in the pipeline, she would be too busy working to worry about her own problems.

They'd agreed to meet at a pub with a very good restaurant a few miles out into the countryside. Ali had told Liz that she'd probably go straight home from there as, knowing John, he'd bring a whole file of documents to their lunch which he'd expect her to have read by Monday morning. However, John appeared to have nothing with him as he rose to greet her in the restaurant. Normally, he'd have pushed aside the cutlery and covered the table with a large plan before she'd even sat down.

Today he seemed a little reserved which, for him, was still loud enough to make several of the other diners look round and the restaurant manager to hover anxiously. It was unlike John Drake not to come straight to the point and, as he uncharacteristically chatted about the weather, Ali started to fear that he'd got some dreadful news, that he was seriously ill or something and she realised how very sad she'd be if that was the case. When he did finally get round to telling her what the problem was, Ali's first response was one of relief. It wasn't until she was driving back to Emma's that she realised how much it would affect her.

"The thing is, Ali," he said, "the property market's fucked at the moment. We can't shift the bastard houses we've got and so there's no sodding point in building more. The fuckers at the bank won't fund us anyway; not on any realistic terms. It's unfuckingbelievable what rates they're offering now.

"So, I said to the wife, let's take six months off, a year maybe, and go travelling. We've spent enough on sending the sodding kids round the world on bloody gap years, why don't we do it ourselves. I've money in the bank earning fuck all interest, I may as well spend it and enjoy ourselves."

Stuck in the Friday afternoon traffic, Ali ran some calculations in her head. The loss of Drake Developments' fees would hit Cassell Brookes and Little hard. Even if John Drake came back sooner than he planned, it would take a while before the work got back to its previous level. For Ali personally, it meant that 50% of her workload would disappear. She'd have to go out and generate some new income, which was difficult enough when every solicitor in town was chasing an ever decreasing pot of business and seemingly impossible when she felt as tired and dispirited as she did currently.

It was Emma who first put the idea into her head. They were sitting in Emma's garden later that evening and Ali was telling her friend about the lunch.

"Why don't you take some time off too, Ali? Have a sabbatical of, say, six months. With no work from Drake Developments your assistant can easily cover your other clients. It would be a good opportunity for her and you could easily be available online if there were any problems. You could travel; go abroad maybe…"

"But what would I live on, Em? I've become used to having a good income. I'm not sure that I could live without it."

"Of course you could. It would only be for six months or so. You must have money in the bank. You could live for a month on what you now earn in a week, two months if you stay away from Waitrose and cut your own hair."

Ali laughed, but the idea of doing something completely different for a while, in a new location, was appealing and, for the first time in weeks, she felt that she could look at her future, if not with hope, then without abject despair.

The next morning Ali met Lucy at the station and suggested that they go for a coffee in the High Street. She had to break the news straight away, before she lost her nerve, and didn't want to do so at Emma's cottage and have Lucy forever afterwards associate it with sorrow. Ordering two flat whites, Ali steered Lucy to a quiet table at the rear. They spoke for a while about Lucy's end of year exams and her plans for the summer.

"I haven't really decided yet, Mum. I'd like to go away somewhere but I need to earn some money first so I guess I'll stay at home with you and Dad. Maybe I can get a job at The Feathers."

This was the opening that Ali had been waiting for; waiting for and dreading.

"Darling, there's something I have to tell you." God, this was difficult, she thought. "I found out quite recently that your Dad has been having an affair. It's over now, at least I think it is, but apparently it wasn't the first time; he's done it before."

Lucy had gone white. She stared blankly at her mother, "Are you sure, Mum? Who told you? I just don't believe Dad would do anything like that." Lucy's face brightened: "You must have got it wrong. It is probably just some village gossip. You know what they are like."

Ali hated to see the hope fade in her daughter's eyes as she said, "I'm sorry, love, but it's true. Your Dad told me himself of the recent affair and the other woman's mother came to my office. That one had been going on for months, apparently. She didn't know he was married and she was very upset when she found out."

Ali didn't want to tell her daughter that the woman had tried to kill herself.

"But Dad did tell you about the last one, and he ended it, didn't he? So he's obviously very sorry."

Ali's sister Linda had, by now, told her that she had seen Jack with Sarah Hill and Ali knew that Jack would never have admitted to the affair unless he'd been forced to do so. She gently explained this to Lucy. Her daughter's eyes filled with tears, "Oh, Mum, I'm so sorry. How could he do this to you? You're so wonderful and beautiful."

At Lucy's words, Ali started to cry as well. She put her arm around her daughter and they walked out of the coffee shop and down to the river.

"What are you going to do, Mum? Will you get a

divorce?"

Whilst Lucy had several friends whose parents were divorced or separated, she had never imagined saying this to her own mother.

"I'm not sure yet, love but, yes, I think so. I've been staying at Emma's for the last week or so. I'm sorry I didn't tell you but I wanted to wait until we were together."

Ali sat on a bench with Lucy beside her. Although it was difficult for her to speak positively of Jack, turning to see her daughter's stricken face, she said, "Whatever your Dad has done, it doesn't mean that he doesn't love you or that he hasn't been a good father. You are everything to him, Luce, you always have been from the moment you were born."

"I feel so angry with him, Mum. I certainly don't want to be at home with him for the summer. Do you think Emma would let me stay at hers with you?"

Ali thought of Emma's immaculate cottage, a refuge at the end of her long working day and the disruption which Ali's own presence had already caused.

"Well, let's take it day by day shall we? I'm not sure that I feel up to the shops, do you? Shall we just go back and sit in Emma's garden? Later on, if you want to, you can call your Dad and talk things through. I know that he'll be hoping to hear from you."

Walking back to Emma's, Ali was relieved that she'd now told Lucy but the fact that her own words had caused her daughter to cry would haunt Ali for a very long time. What misery Jack had caused. She hoped that he appreciated all she was doing to prevent Lucy seeing him as she now did.

Ali left Lucy in the garden with Emma whilst she went into the kitchen to cook them all a meal. She hoped that Lucy would be able to say things to Emma that she couldn't tell her mother. She just hoped that Emma wouldn't be too scathing about Jack. Well, perhaps a little criticism wouldn't hurt. Ali wanted Lucy to have a good relationship with her father but it was Jack who was responsible for making that happen, not her.

It had been more than a week since Mrs Keeling came to her office and, as Ali chopped peppers and mushrooms for a sauce, she examined her feelings about Jack. She felt very differently to how she had when he'd told her of his affair with Sarah Hill. Then, although sickened by what he'd done, she was still connected to him; he remained her Jack. Now, it was as if she'd never really known him at all. It seemed incomprehensible that the man she loved and had spent years of her life with, would do the treacherous things that he had.

She knew that her marriage was over. She felt so angry with him for so carelessly throwing away her love and, by choosing to sleep with other women, stealing from her the confidence and belief she had in herself. Not only had he taken away all of her hopes and plans for the future, he had stolen her memories as well; the happy marriage that she had been so proud of had been nothing but a sham.

In the garden, Lucy was saying something similar to Emma: "I just feel as though my childhood memories have been trashed, Em. I thought that my Dad really loved my Mum and me, but he couldn't have or he wouldn't have done this to us."

"He does love you, Lucy. Remember that always. He may be a shit husband but he's still your Dad. Everyone makes mistakes, he's just made a few more than most; a lot more in fact."

Emma couldn't quite believe that she was making excuses for Jack's behaviour.

"Come on, let's see how your Mum's getting on in the kitchen. If she's burnt my copper bottomed pans, I'll kill her."

After dinner Lucy went upstairs to call her Dad and came down looking pale but composed. Although she'd clearly been crying, she was now dry eyed and she met her mother's worried look with a small smile.

"How did it go? You don't have to tell us if you don't want to," added Ali hurriedly.

"It's OK, Mum," said Lucy, coming to sit with Ali on the sofa. "He kept saying how sorry he was. He was crying, it was awful really. I said that I'd meet him next week. You don't mind, do you?"

"Of course not, darling. That's what I want; I told you that. Are you going to see him at home?"

"That's the thing, Mum. Dad said that he'd go and stay at Uncle Peter's for a bit, so that you and I can go back to the cottage. Unless you'd rather stay here with Emma? I'll be fine at home on my own."

"No, we'll go back together. We can drive there tomorrow morning. I'm sure Emma will be glad to have her own space again, hey, Em?"

Emma, unloading the dishwasher to find one of her favourite glasses had been cracked, could only agree.

CHAPTER FIFTEEN

It felt strange to be back in her own home again but in such different circumstances. Most of Jack's things had gone from the bathroom and Ali walked around the cottage gathering the rest; a half read book next to their bed, a jumper on a kitchen chair and put everything away in his wardrobe out of sight. Whilst she was sorting, she took her turquoise dress downstairs. She'd take it to the charity shop in Barton Casey on Monday; she never wanted to wear it again.

The week passed more quickly than Ali had expected. She was busy at work dealing with the property side of a major corporate deal. Ali's job was to complete title reports on twenty commercial units to give to the bank's solicitors and she'd been at her desk by seven most mornings and not leaving until ten or twelve hours later.

In the evenings, if Lucy was home, they'd sit and watch TV together. They were currently halfway through a box set of an American crime series and often had to force themselves not to watch it late into the night. However, Lucy was often out in the evenings. Ali was glad to note that the girls Lucy had abandoned for Mason had not seemed to have taken offence and she'd come home from work to find the TV blaring away in an empty sitting room and the garden full of laughing girls.

Lucy appeared to be fine. She'd gone to meet her father midweek and, although she hadn't said much on her return, and Ali hadn't pressed her, she seemed happy enough. Unfortunately, there were no jobs to be had at The Feathers or anywhere else. Ali was surprised then to see Lucy wearing new jeans and sandals and, when she asked about them, her daughter grinned, "Dad gave me some money. Guilt money, of course but, hey, shoes are shoes." Her face fell: "Oh, you don't mind do you, Mum? I haven't upset you have I? I can give it back."

Lucy started pulling notes from the pocket of her jeans.

"You keep it, love. He'd have given you money anyway. You know how he always spoils you."

The conversation about money made Ali think and, when Lucy went out that evening, she sat in the study and began to do some calculations.

"Do you know," said Sarah Hill as she handed her husband a gin and tonic, "Mrs Keeling is acting really strangely. She turned up to clean this morning wearing a sort of evening dress. Turquoise it was. I saw a similar one in LDB, you know, that shop I like in the High Street. This would have been a copy of course. She couldn't afford their prices, even on what I pay her."

Chris Hill made suitable noises. He wasn't really listening. He was still reliving his recent golf match with Jack Jones when he'd beaten him, quite convincingly, for the first time. Jack's game seemed to have gone to pot, he'd never seen him play so badly.

Sarah was still talking, "And she completely ruined my cream silk blouse. There's a scorch mark on the sleeve where she's had the iron too hot. I may have to let her go. What do you think darling?"

But Chris, engrossed in his memories of sinking that putt on the seventeenth, hardly heard her. Perhaps he'd speak to the pro about a few lessons on his swing; he'd love to see Jack's face if he beat him again this Sunday.

It was Linda who found Lucy a job. The council, where Linda worked, were looking for temporary office assistants to cover the holiday period and Linda said that she and Carl would love it if Lucy came to stay for a while.

"Are you sure, Lin?" said Ali. "Have you forgotten what it was like to be nineteen? You'll never be able to get in the bathroom and she'd cut off her hand rather than let go of her phone."

"It will be nice for Carl to have someone nearer his own age to play with," Linda joked, "and I can take Lucy shopping. There's a place just down the road that has these amazing tartan leggings; Lucy will love it."

"Actually, it might work out quite well." Ali paused. "I haven't spoken to the other partners yet but I may take some time off work."

"Yes, why don't you. A few weeks holiday would do you good."

"No, I was thinking of longer, six months maybe. I may go abroad."

As both Emma and Linda seemed to be in favour of her plans, Ali resolved to speak to her senior partner on Monday morning. First, however, she needed to see how Lucy felt about it all.

Lucy was all for it: "Definitely go for it, Mum. I've been so worried about you, how you'll cope when I go back to uni. It would be fantastic for you to go off and do something exciting."

Ali could see that, whilst she'd been concerned about Lucy, her sensitive and caring daughter had been thinking of her and that the best thing she could do for Lucy right now was to make her believe that her mother was fine.

On Sunday evening Ali called Carolyn. She hadn't spoken to her for a few weeks. Although Ali knew that she was being unfair, she slightly blamed Carolyn for bringing Sarah Hill into their lives.

"Ali, I'd meant to phone you. Just a second." Ali could hear the sound of a door shutting "That's better. Now, how are you coping darling?"

Ali wasn't surprised that Carolyn knew what had happened. Not a lot escaped the village grapevine.

"How did you hear?"

"Well, Jack told us." Her voice sounded hesitant. "Actually, he's here now. Trevor saw him at the golf club and asked him back for supper. Look, I know what he did was wrong, Ali, but the poor bloke is distraught. I'm sure if the two of you sit down together and talk it through, have some counselling maybe, you can work this out."

Carolyn's voice became bolder and a note of

excitement crept in, "Tell me, how did you find out about Mrs Keeling's daughter? Did you find something in Jack's pockets or a message on his phone?"

Ali felt furious, "As you have clearly become Jack's best friend, I suggest you ask him about it. I'm surprised at you, Carolyn. I can understand, just, Trevor being on Jack's side but you, well, quite honestly I feel betrayed. I don't want to talk about this anymore," and she rang off.

Ali had never understood before why, when couples split up, their friends seemed to divide into two camps; they were for one side or the other, never both. Knowing that Carolyn and Trevor had invited Jack into their home and worse, that Carolyn appeared to view Jack's behaviour as some sort of laddish prank, the details of which she could salaciously enjoy, hurt Ali deeply and she doubted that her friendship with Carolyn would ever fully recover.

Carolyn put the phone down but stood with her hand still on the receiver for a few moments. Ali had never spoken to her so sharply before; it was almost as though she hated her. Carolyn thought about what she'd said. She didn't deserve Ali's words, surely? She remembered Jack mentioning something about Ali hitting the wine quite hard recently and gave a sign of relief. That would be it; she was probably drunk. All the same, when Carolyn went back into the dining room to join the men, she felt irritated by their laddish good humour and was snappy with them both for the rest of the meal.

She continued to worry about her friend for the rest of the evening and later, in bed, she turned towards Trevor and kissed him, glad of his solid presence beside her. Trevor was surprised at this display of affection after her frosty demeanour at dinner. *Blimey*, he thought, *it's not even Saturday night.*

CHAPTER SIXTEEN

She'd done it. She'd arranged with Cassell Brookes and Little that she would take a six-month sabbatical, starting in two weeks' time. Her current clients would be looked after by her assistant and, when the new trainees started in September, they could help out. Ali had readily agreed to be available on the phone or online whenever necessary.

Mr Little had tried hard to persuade Ali to change her mind. She was very fond of him and his wife Rosemary and, although she had intended not to, had found herself telling him everything that had happened with Jack.

"I know that I will have to build up my client base when I return. If my assistant Amanda looks after my clients in the way I think she will, I don't expect that I'll find it easy to get them back. But I did it before when I started here and I know I can do it again, just not right now – right now I need to get away."

Ali had decided that, as she had six months to herself, she'd try to do something useful with her time and learn a new skill. After discounting several options, she thought that what she'd really like was to learn a language properly. The idea of returning to Compesita appealed to her. She already knew a few people there and if she wanted to move to somewhere else after a few months, then she could.

She worked out that, if she was careful with her budget, she could support herself for six months on what she had in her back account plus half of what she and Jack had saved towards a holiday. They had planned to go to Saint Lucia in January but clearly they would not be going now.

Now that matters were settled with Cassell Brookes and Little, Ali began to feel quite excited. It was daunting, of course, to go abroad by herself and for such a long time but she hoped that Emma, Linda and Lucy would come out and visit. Time would probably fly by.

The problems with Mason had meant that Lucy hadn't yet found anywhere to live when she returned to Bath in September. They had looked at various sites which advertised rooms in student houses and Jack had suggested that he drive Lucy over that weekend to view some places. Ali had felt disappointed that she couldn't go as well as, or instead of Jack, but she didn't want to see him and, having encouraged her daughter to remain close to her father, she could hardly veto their trip now.

"Just make sure that you chose a nice, safe area, Lucy. It doesn't matter about the house itself, you can always make your room pretty with lamps and cushions and things but you want somewhere fairly decent. Your father can afford it. He pays enough for his golf club membership."

Let Jack pay out as much as possible, thought Ali grimly. It was the least he could do.

"OK, Mum, I will. I wish you were coming too though. I'll take some videos on my phone to show you."

With Lucy away for the weekend with Jack, alone in the cottage Ali found her spirits dropping. Her marriage was over and now she'd given up her job; could she really cope in a foreign country without her friends and family to support her?

She read again the email she'd received from Jack that morning. She'd sent one to him explaining her plans and telling him that she was taking half of their holiday money. She added that she expected he'd be glad to move back into the cottage and finished by saying that she knew he'd keep a close eye on Lucy.

Jack had sent her a long email in reply. He'd said that she was the love of his life and that he didn't think that he'd ever recover from losing her. He added that he knew it was completely his fault; he couldn't explain why he'd done what he did but that he was going to try very hard to be a better man. He'd assured her that he would take care of Lucy and thanked Ali for not turning their daughter against him. He told her to take all of the holiday money they'd saved and ended by telling her that he knew how much he'd hurt her and that if she ever needed him, for anything at all, he would be there.

Jack's words made Ali cry. What a waste it all was, what a stupid waste. To make Ali feel worse, Dionne Warwick was bemoaning lost love on the radio. Come on, she thought, this won't do. She found something more upbeat and spent a pleasant few minutes considering what to do with Jack's holiday money; an extra £3,500. She could rent a car now or even buy a cheap one. She could pay for Lucy to fly out and visit her and she'd keep the rest for essentials, such as vodka.

"Well I'm sorry, Mrs Jones, but it is high season now and that's the cheapest rental I have in Compesita. Villa Olivia, where you stayed last time, would be twice that price."

Ali was disappointed. She realised that rental prices would be higher in the peak summer months but not the astronomical sums the letting agent was quoting. It looked like she would have to change her plans.

"It's just you, is it? On your own again?"

Well the bloody woman doesn't have to rub it in, thought Ali.

"It's just that, if you don't mind coping without air conditioning, I may have something for you. It's very small, just two rooms and a shower really, although there is a pretty little patio garden. The owners are selling but if you would show the occasional buyer round and are flexible about the notice period, I think they'd be happy to let it to you. It's not on the rental website but if you look under sales you'll see it. It's called Casa Lucia."

Hastily revising her opinion of the letting agent, Ali eagerly logged on to the website. The villa looked impossibly tiny in the photographs (and so was probably even smaller in reality), but the price was reasonable and she'd taken the name as a good omen. She called the agent back and agreed to rent it on a rolling monthly basis.

Ali lay in bed unable to sleep. Had she made the right

decision? Would it have been better if she'd buried herself in her work or should she have tried to forgive Jack; gone to counselling as Carolyn had suggested? No, she was certain that her marriage was over. She just felt impossibly sad and her instincts were telling her that, in order to heal herself, to recover, she needed to get away, away from the stress of her job, away from the cottage with its echoes of Jack. Casa Lucia would help her, she felt sure of it.

Linda walked out of the surgery in tears. People in the waiting room stared at her and one woman got up and touched her arm saying: "Are you OK, dear? Bad news was it?" But Linda didn't answer.

At first she couldn't remember where she'd parked her car, there were never any spaces near the surgery but, after twice walking in the wrong direction, she found it and sat inside, clutching the car keys and tried to steady her breathing.

The doctor had been very kind and said that she knew it must be a shock. She explained that there were lots of non-invasive tests they could do these days and that Linda must try not to worry. She added that the hospital would be in touch very soon and the best thing Linda could do now was to go home and rest.

Opening her front door, Linda could hear music and, looking down the hall, saw Carl in the kitchen. He had a pile of exercise books on the table in front of him and was writing comments in his small neat hand. How he could concentrate with his iPod blasting away was beyond her. She called to him but he didn't hear her. When she touched his arm he looked up in surprise and turned off the music.

"Sorry, love, what did you say?"

Linda's voice sounded very loud in the silence of the room, "I said I'm pregnant," and she burst into tears.

Sitting on the sofa later with a cup of tea and her feet on Carl's lap, Linda smiled, "I have an awful feeling that you're going to be one of those annoyingly involved men who come to every antenatal class and ask a lot of difficult questions."

"Oh, much worse than that," grinned Carl (he hadn't stopped grinning for the past hour), "I'm going to get a prosthetic stomach so I can identify with your changing body shape. I'll have sympathy pains when you go into labour and you'll be abandoned whilst the nurses tend to my needs. And, of course, from now on I will only address you as Mother."

They'd never really discussed having a child. Linda's periods had always been erratic and had almost stopped by the time she'd met Carl and so she'd assumed that she'd had an early menopause. She'd felt guilty that he'd never be a father and, although he often came home from the large secondary school where he taught maths with stories of the horrendous behaviour of his pupils ("Britney Davies bit David Marshall today, she actually drew blood. You think she'd have a bit more respect, he is the headmaster."), Linda knew that he adored children and was very good with them. His class worshipped him.

"Tell me again what the GP said about tests and things."

Although Carl didn't say it, Linda knew that he was as concerned as she was about her age.

"Well, she said that at forty-seven I am, of course, quite old to be having my first child. She used some awful Latin term that I can't remember but which obviously meant a woman who is too old and fat to be having sex, let alone a baby. She did say that, these days, they can get a lot of information just from blood tests. If those tests show signs of, well, of anything wrong" – Linda couldn't bring herself to say abnormality – "then I can have amniocentesis. Although that brings its own risk, of course.

"She did say that I appear to be healthy and there is no reason why I shouldn't have a perfectly normal baby. She asked how old you were. She seemed quite impressed when I told her, I think she was expecting me to say that my husband was ninety-six."

Carl leaned over and kissed her: "We'll take it one step at a time, love. Whatever you decide to do about tests, is OK with me. We don't have to have any at all if you don't want to. What I'm really worried about is do you think we should call it Enid or Ethel? Only if it's a boy, of course. I was thinking Pinot for a girl. What do you think, Mother?"

CHAPTER SEVENTEEN

Ali had driven to Tarea, a town about five miles from Compesita to stock up on bottled water and other supplies which were difficult to carry from the village shop. She was having coffee before going back when a man stopped at her table.

"It's Alison isn't it? Hi, I'm Paul, do you remember? It's nice to see you again."

Ali did remember, he was the guy who had rescued her from the drunken advances of that awful man at the beach bar.

"Call me Ali please. I've just ordered a coffee. Do you have time to join me? Is your sister with you?"

Paul sat down at Ali's table and waved to the waiter. Ali smiled at him. He looked different somehow. He saw her looking and stroked his chin.

"I've shaved my beard off. Three people bought me aftershave for my birthday and so I took the hint."

"I like it," said Ali and she did. Clean faced, his hazel eyes seemed more intense and she noticed that he had a slight cleft in his chin. As had happened the last time she had seen him in the village bar, she felt a pull of attraction towards him.

"My sister's not with me this time. I'm staying at her place though. It's a mile or so from Compesita. Are you in Casa Olivia still?"

Ali didn't feel like telling Paul everything that had happened since she last saw him so she briefly told him that she was still in Compesita and then changed the subject. If he noticed that she was being evasive, he made no sign of it but instead entertained her with a story about the Spanish cleaning lady at his sister Jan's villa, who was determined to marry him off to her daughter.

"I was walking past the local bar the other night and, you know how all the local men sit together outside? Well, Paco (he's the father of my intended) calls me over and he stands up and makes this long speech (in Spanish of course) and I have to go round the table shaking hands with all of the men. They all started slapping me on the back and calling me Hombre. I'm dreading going near the church in case I see a notice about the bans."

Ali laughed: "And what's she like, this fiancée of yours?"

"She's about fifteen stone and has a better beard than I had. She does have lovely eyes though. I've got a thing about eyes," Paul stared into Ali's for a moment, "and Paco's a builder, so I expect he'll build us a house. I can't complain, not really."

"I tell you what," said Ali, "why don't I turn up at Jan's house one day pretending to be your ex-girlfriend who's set on reconciliation? Assuming you do want to get out of the wedding, that is."

"Well, we'd have to give the gifts back and I am rather fond of the set of coasters depicting all twelve disciples but it's not a bad idea. I'd like you to see Jan's house anyway. Why don't you come over tomorrow? If you get there before one, Juanita the cleaner will still be there."

Ali had been in Compesita for three weeks and, whilst she was less lonely than she feared, it would be good to have some company. She also realised that her conversation with Paul was the first time she had relaxed, had laughed even, since she'd arrived. She agreed to be at Jan's house at eleven the next day.

She was delighted with Casa Lucia. It was very small, just two rooms really; a bedroom with a tiny shower cubicle on the ground floor and upstairs a gallery kitchen with a sitting area at the far end. The villa was very plainly furnished but she'd added some colourful rugs and pottery that she'd bought locally and, when the lamps were lit in the evenings, it looked enchanting.

Ali found that her days had fallen into a routine. She went for a walk in the early mornings, whilst it was still cool, stopping at the bakery for a fresh loaf to have with her breakfast coffee. After a few hours listening to her Spanish CDs, Ali would take her laptop to one of the bars in the main square and check her emails. Sometimes she'd Skype Lucy, who was having a great time at Linda's, although she was finding her job at the council very dull. In the afternoons, she'd have a siesta and then take a book into the sunny patio garden at the front of the villa and read until she felt hungry.

Ali had never particularly enjoyed cooking for just herself but now she looked forward to this part of the day the most. Emma had given her a Spanish cookery book before she left and Ali would put on some music, pour her first glass of wine of the day and experiment with a selection of tapas or perhaps a chicken and chorizo casserole. Some of her efforts were more successful than others but she usually enjoyed her meals, eaten at a tiny iron table in the garden, with her music drifting softly from an open window.

There was no TV or internet and she found she didn't miss it. It would be different if the weather was rainy or cold but here she could sit in the garden until it went dark or go for a walk. She'd gradually got to know the village, turning down the narrow streets at random until she'd find herself back once again in the main square. Occasionally, Ali would stop during her evening rambles and have a coffee and a brandy in one of the bars before walking slowly back to Casa Lucia. She tried not to drink too much as she found that, whilst one brandy made her feel brave and self-congratulatory, after two or three she became tearful and bitter. Even without alcohol her mood changed often during each day; one minute she'd be enjoying a stroll through the village when the sight of something, a couple holding hands or a car the same colour as Jack's, would plunge her into utter despair and she'd find that, almost without being aware of it, she was crying.

The morning after seeing Paul in the café, Ali set off in her hired Twingo. It was rather old but she'd taken it for a month at a very good rate. Stopping once or twice to read the directions Paul had written down for her, she eventually saw a sign for Villa Almonzora, with an arrow pointing to the right. Taking the turning, the road came to a dead end by a set of very grand double gates.

Ali left her car in the road and walked up the drive. *Jan and her husband must be very wealthy as the house in front of her would look more in place in Marbella than a dusty village*, she thought. It was very modern, with lots of glass and clean, straight lines. The garden was laid to gravel, interspersed with tall feathery plants and, here and there, large marble boulders.

Paul stepped out of the massive wooden front door and shouted, "Ali, what on earth are you doing here?" Looking back over his shoulder into the hallway he added: "It's over I tell you. It's over."

Ali stared at him. Surely he'd remembered that he'd asked her to come? She really shouldn't be here in the middle of nowhere with a man she hardly knew. She turned to leave.

"You're my ex-girlfriend now. Have you forgotten that?" Paul called urgently.

Of course, Ali recalled their conversation at the café. She was supposed to be his ex, come for reconciliation. Oh well, he'd asked for it. She ran up to Paul and, spying a small dark-haired woman hovering in the hall behind him, flung her arms around his neck and kissed him deeply on the mouth. She then dropped to her knees and hugged his legs (God, she was enjoying this).

"I love you, Paul. I can't live without you any longer. I'm sorry that I, err, I'm sorry that I slept with your father." Ali felt Paul's legs starting to shake, "And your grandfather." Paul let out a snort. "But I want you to forgive me. Please, please say that you will."

Paul handed Ali a glass of Cava.

"Sorry I've been so long but I had to wash the glasses. Juanita went off in a huff without turning the dishwasher on. I hope she calms down. Jan will never forgive me if I lose her cleaner." He looked into her eyes. "It must have been the kiss that did it. Juanita wouldn't have understood what you said, her English isn't good."

"Oh well," said Ali. "Your father taught me everything I know. Anyway, Juanita will get over it. She'll realise what a lucky escape her daughter's had when she hears your taste in music." Dolly Parton was singing lustily in the background.

"Come on, you can't beat a bit of Country and Western. I think it's the song titles that do it for me. My favourite is 'My Girlfriend's Run Off With Grandpa; Oh How I Miss The Old Guy'."

Ali giggled: "How about, 'I Get A Funny Feeling When You Kiss Me. I Think It Must Be Your Beard'."

They spent the rest of the afternoon making up ever more unlikely song titles. When she left, Paul walked her to her car and, leaning in through the open window, kissed her softly on the lips. He stroked his hand briefly over her hair before saying, "What a lovely day. I'll see you very soon."

As Ali pulled up outside Casa Lucia she realised that, for the first time in weeks, she hadn't thought about Jack once all day.

CHAPTER EIGHTEEN

Emma was late leaving the bank due to a panic over the Yen and the wine bar was packed by the time she arrived. She pushed through the chattering hoards and spotted Simon sitting at a table at the back. A very pretty girl with a long fringe almost covering her eyes was sitting next to him.

"Em, this is Cici; Cici, Emma Brown, my oldest friend."

Simon got up and gave Emma a kiss.

Simon had talked about his latest girlfriend for weeks but this was the first time that Emma had met her. She looked very young, much younger than Simon and Emma wondered, not for the first time, how he managed to get a seemingly unending string of attractive young women to go out with him.

Cici beamed at Emma, "I've heard so much about you. I couldn't wait to meet you. I know that we're going to be great friends."

Simon's girlfriends were either icily dismissive of Emma or gushingly overfriendly. Cici's smile, however, appeared to be quite genuine and she gazed at Emma with steady blue eyes.

"I'm fairly new to London. I'm a bit of a country girl actually. My family can't bear the city and think I'm mad to have moved here. I do miss the farm though, especially the animals." Cici turned and took hold of Simon's hand. "It's just so fab that Si and I both simply adore horses and dogs."

Emma stared at Simon. She knew quite well that dogs scared him and that he'd never been near a horse in his life.

"Remind me," Emma said, "what was the name of that black stallion you used to ride around Hyde Park? Gladiator wasn't it? Perhaps you could take Cici to see him?"

"Wow, I've always wanted to ride on Rotten Row. Oh, do let's, Si. We could go tomorrow."

"I can't, honey pie. I hurt my back playing polo a few weeks ago. It's not something I talk about, I don't like to complain."

Emma wondered what other lies Simon had told to Cici. Part of his charm was his ability to fit into any setting; unfortunately, this often meant that he stretched the truth somewhat.

"Actually, Em, we have some news for you." Simon paused and squeezed Cici's hand. "We are going to get married. Isn't that wonderful?"

Emma now saw that on the third finger of Cici's childlike hand was a beautiful square cut diamond ring.

"It was exactly what I would have chosen myself."

Emma had called Ali as soon as she got home. It was 11.30pm in Spain and Ali had been in bed, reading.

"How do you feel, Em?" asked Ali anxiously. She was hoping that her friend would move on now that Simon was undeniably unavailable but she feared that Emma wouldn't see it that way.

"I feel as though my life is over." Emma sighed: "I knew it would happen one day but I just kept hoping, you know? He wants me to be his best woman. We're to wear matching Ozwald Boateng suits. Well, I can't look any worse than I did at your wedding."

Ali laughed. They'd been short of money and she'd bought Emma a bottle green bridesmaid's dress in the Laura Ashley sale.

"What's she like, this Cici?"

"She's lovely actually. Much too good for him."

"Why don't you come out and stay with me for a bit?" Ali asked. "It would do you good. Somehow just being here has helped me a lot."

Emma said that she'd see if she could get some time off work and the friends said goodnight.

It was true that being in Compesita, in little Casa Lucia,

was helping Ali to recover. Whilst she couldn't say that she was happy, she no longer felt a constant aching sadness. She'd made some friends as well with a couple who were upbeat and uncomplicated; exactly the companions she needed right now. She'd been having a drink in one of the bars in the square, as she sometimes did in the evenings, when the couple on the next table caught her attention; they seemed to be having such a good time. The woman was very blonde and tanned and she wore a white dress that looked deceptively simple and very expensive. The man was stocky with closely cropped hair and deep set blue eyes.

They were laughing because the man had ordered something which turned out to be a single large octopus tentacle, covered in suckers.

"Blimey, looks like something from a horror movie. Oh my God, what's the waiter bringing now!"

When the woman turned to look, the man speared a large forkful of chicken from her plate.

Seeing Ali smile, they began to talk to her and the three of them stayed drinking and chatting until the waiters began to stack up the chairs beside them and they reluctantly rose to leave.

Lee had introduced her partner Des: "We're not married yet. We've only been together for twenty-five years and I'm still not sure about him," she said, looking at him fondly. They had rented a villa in the village for the summer. Lee had told Ali that they had their own printing business but their son more or less ran it now. Finding out that Ali was on her own, they immediately began to make plans for her.

"Have you been to the Pilates class in the community centre?" Lee asked Ali. "Oh, it's good. That's on Mondays and they do Zumba on Thursdays."

Des wanted Ali to go walking with him. "Lee won't come, she's frightened of seeing snakes. You should come, Ali. A group of us go every Wednesday. It's amazing when you get up into the hills, you can see for miles."

By the end of the evening Ali found that she had agreed to go to their villa for lunch the next day and that her Monday, Wednesday and Thursday mornings were booked up for the next six weeks.

A few days later, Ali had arranged to Skype Lucy at 7pm UK time but, when she went into the bar and logged on she was surprised to see Lucy, Linda and Carl all squashed together on Linda's sofa. All three were grinning broadly. Lucy said, "Auntie Lin's got some news, Mum."

And at the same time, Linda shrieked, "I'm pregnant, Ali. I'm going to have a baby."

Linda explained that she'd had some blood tests and that everything looked absolutely normal. "I've had to give up the fags though. I had to with these two watching my every move. Oh and it's a girl, so we're going to call her Laura, after Mum." (Ali and Linda's Mum had died a couple of years ago, quickly followed by their Dad.)

"Oh, Linda, Carl, that's the best news I've had in ages. I'm so, so happy for you."

Linda and Carl disappeared from the screen although Ali could hear Carl in the background saying in an exaggerated Leeds accent, "Now then, Mother, hows about a nice cuppa?"

Lucy told Ali about the flat she'd found near the university: "It's on a bus route. I'll be sharing with three others. I haven't met them yet but we've messaged and they all seem really nice. Oh and, Mum, I saw Mason the other day."

Ali's heart sank. Her warning to Mason to stay away obviously hadn't worked.

"I'd gone back home to go to Adele's party and I was at the station when I saw him on the platform. He looked terrified and said, 'Don't tell your Mum you've seen me,' and he jumped onto a train which had just come in. I think it was going to Edinburgh." Lucy laughed. "I do hope it was a nonstop one. He looked really skanky, Mum. What on earth did I ever see in him?"

As she walked back from the bar Ali couldn't help smiling. The news about Linda's baby was the first good news she'd received for ages and Ali hoped that it was a sign that everything was going to get just a little bit better from now on. She knew that Linda had always wanted to have a child but she'd never found the right man until she met Carl and by then they'd both assumed that she'd had an early menopause and it was too late. Ali was concerned about Linda's age though. She decided to do some research online; there may be some vitamins or particular foods that older mothers should take and she could order them to be sent to Linda. She wasn't going to look into the risks or statistics. There was no point and Ali was determined that this baby was going to be a positive event; the beginning of a new, happier era.

CHAPTER NINETEEN

Ali had bought a paella pan at the local market and was shopping for ingredients when she saw Paul. On impulse she invited him round that evening.

"I've never made paella before so it will probably turn out like savoury porridge. I know that you're not really supposed to eat it in the evening but I thought, what the hell, let's go bonkers."

Preparing the meal later that day Ali wondered if she'd made a mistake. What if Paul read too much into the invitation and pounced on her. She really wasn't ready to have a relationship with another man, although the kiss they'd had certainly stirred something inside her. She poured herself a vodka and tonic and began to peel the prawns.

Was paella supposed to be this runny, Ali thought, peering at her recipe book. It looked more like soup. She threw in another handful of rice and sipped the wine she had opened, stirring hopefully.

In the end, the paella turned out rather well. Ali had decorated it with whole prawns and lemon quarters and it looked, if not quite tasted, exactly like the photograph in the book. She and Paul sat outside at the little iron table and when it grew dark Ali lit some candles and carried out a pot of coffee.

"I think I'll have a brandy with mine. How about you?"

Paul refused, as he was driving; he'd drunk only beer with his meal. Emboldened by the wine and brandy and encouraged by the intimacy of the candle lit garden, Ali asked Paul to tell her more about himself. Up to now their conversation had been light and inconsequential.

"Well, when I left the SAS I was a racing driver for a while but I found that those little white hood things they wear under their helmets tickled my beard so I quit."

"No, seriously, Paul. I don't know anything about you. Were you, are you, married?"

Paul poured himself another coffee. "I was married, yes, but it didn't work out. We've been divorced for years."

"Any children?"

"I have a daughter of eighteen. She's called Ella." Paul looked down at his hands. " I haven't seen her since she was eight."

Ali gasped. She tried to imagine never seeing Lucy; the thought was abhorrent.

"Why ever not? If you don't mind talking about it, that is."

"Oh, I expect I was a very bad father. I was certainly a bad husband. My ex-wife and I were very young when we got together. I was twenty-two when we married and we had Ella two years later. I was working very hard at the university, finishing my PhD and starting to do some lecturing at the same time. We had virtually no money and it wasn't the life that Karen, my ex, had envisaged. She was depressed and lonely and we argued all of the time. One day I came home to find that Karen had left with Ella. My daughter was about two then."

"But didn't you try to keep in contact with Ella?"

"Of course I did. Karen had moved back up North to be near her parents. At first I went up every weekend but it was so expensive that I began going less often. Then Karen met and married someone else. Ella was only four.

"They didn't want me in her life; she had a new Daddy. They made it very difficult for me to see her. I'd go all the way up there and they wouldn't be in or Karen would say that Ella was ill and couldn't leave the house."

"But, Paul, as the father you had legal rights. You could have gone to Court and got an order."

"I did go down that route but, in the meantime, they moved house and it took me ages to find them. By the time I'd got a Judge to award me contact rights, Ella hardly knew me. She used to scream when I came to take her out for the day; she used to scream for her other Daddy.

"In the end I thought it would be better for Ella if I

stayed away; stayed out of her life."

"Oh, Paul, I'm so sorry." He looked so tired and sad that Ali leant forward and put her hand on his arm.

"I comforted myself with the thought that, when she got older, she'd want to find out about her real father and she'd contact me. She's eighteen now and I'm still waiting. I don't suppose she ever will now." Paul shook his head, "Anyway, that's enough about me. Tell me your story, Ali. What brought you to Spain?"

Ali got another brandy and, sitting in the fragrant solitude of Casa Lucia's little garden, told Paul everything that had happened with Jack. It was nearly 2am before Paul stood up to leave. He helped Ali carry the glasses and cups into the house. In the kitchen Ali stumbled slightly and, when Paul caught her arm, she pressed herself against him and lifted her face to be kissed. He brushed his lips gently on hers before pulling away.

"This isn't a good idea, Ali. You've had quite a bit to drink and we've both had an emotional night. Besides," he smiled, "how do I know you'd respect me in the morning."

Paul kissed Ali on the forehead, told her to sleep well and left.

Ali and Lee were having a coffee after their Zumba class and Lee had wanted to know all about Ali's evening with Paul.

"So he's not much to look at then?"

"Oh, well he's really quite good looking, sexy actually."

"Bit dull then, no conversation to speak of?"

"God no, I feel as though I could talk to him for hours and he's so funny sometimes."

"I expect he's not as clever as you?"

"He's a university lecturer; he's way cleverer than me."

"OK, so there's this hot, witty, clever guy with a good job and you don't want to have a relationship with him because…? What are you looking for; ugly, dull and stupid?"

Ali sighed: "I think it's just too soon, Lee, you know, after Jack. Anyway, I made a complete fool of myself. I tried to kiss him and he pulled away. He obviously doesn't fancy me."

"I wouldn't be so sure about that, Ali. This isn't him coming towards us now, by any chance?"

Paul strolled over to the bar wearing a crisp white linen shirt and navy shorts. Ali fluffed up her hair and Lee looked at her with amusement.

"Hello, ladies, you're looking hot."

"If you mean sweaty, then yes we are. We've just done a Zumba class."

"No, I meant hot," said Paul, gazing at Ali. "I wanted to thank you for last night; to thank you for listening to me. Also to say that I'm going to Granada for a week or so but I'll call you when I get back, if that's OK?" Paul looked a little unsure of himself.

Ali could feel Lee kicking her under the table. "Ouch, err yes, I'd like that very much," and she realised, to her surprise that she would.

Ali was woken by the sound of gunshot. She sat up in bed and listened; there is was again. The village men often went hunting up in the hills but the shots sounded as though they were coming from the village itself. She dressed and walked cautiously up to the main square.

"Ali, come and join us."

Lee and Des were having breakfast outside the corner bar. Ali ordered an orange juice and asked her friends if they'd heard the gunshot. Des laughed, "It's the fireworks. Well, if you can call them that. It's just a series of loud bangs really. It's for the village fiesta. There will be quite a party in the top square tonight. We watched them putting up the stage earlier, didn't we, Lee? We went last year, it was great fun."

"Oh, the little girls dress up and do flamenco dancing and later on there's a band, well, there was last year."

Just at that moment they could hear the divergent tones

111

of the Compestita band turning into the square. It had been parading through the village for weeks, seemingly always to be playing the same tune. Ali recognised a couple of the waiters from the bars and the baker's daughter; they were all ages and not terribly good.

"I'm not sure I could listen to them all night," said Ali grimly.

"Oh no, they do play, of course, but that's earlier. Later on, really late, about midnight, there'll be a proper band, with guitars and a singer. Everyone dances, it'll be great."

Des said that there was no point in going up too early and so Ali agreed to meet them by the church at eleven that evening. As she got ready, Ali could hear the music. It seemed strange to be going out so late. It reminded her of going to clubs with Emma years ago. Emma had called her that afternoon and said that she didn't think she'd have time to come out before the wedding but she'd asked Ali if she would fly back to support her for the big day. Emma had sounded so desperate that Ali found herself agreeing to go.

When she reached the top square just after eleven it was packed. There was a large stage at one end and, opposite, a temporary bar had been set up. The band had yet to appear but the sound system was blasting out Spanish pop music. Lights had been strung between the trees lining the square and grandmothers sat with babies whilst children ran about and teenagers eyed each other shyly. Everyone was dressed up; Ali hardly recognised many of the villagers she'd come to know, they all looked so different and she was glad that she'd put on her floaty red dress and, for the first time in ages, high heels.

Ali saw Ronny and Alan standing by the bar with another man and went over to talk to them.

"Ali, darling girl," cried Alan, kissing her cheek. He and Ronny had, thank goodness, stopped calling her Alison Olivia.

"Let me get you a drink, vodka tonic? Now, this is our dear friend Robert. Robert, Ali."

Ali turned to see a tall slim man with an angular face and green eyes, like her own. He had blonde hair brushed straight back from his forehead and he was extremely good looking.

"Hi, nice to meet you. I'm Robert but just call me Robert."

The man laughed at his own wit but Ronny and Alan looked a little strained and Ali wondered how many times they'd heard this before. Ali had hardly had a chance to sip her drink before a local man grabbed her hand and pulled her onto the dancefloor in front of the stage. Putting one arm around her waist he whirled her energetically into a sort of manic quick step, all the time grinning broadly. The music stopped but he kept hold of her hand and, when another song started seconds later, he sped off with her again.

Three dances later Ali managed to break away and rejoined the others. She laughingly told them that she had tried to tell her dance partner that she was tired but, knowing that the Spanish words for tired and married were very similar, she had an awful feeling that she'd mixed them up.

"I think I've just become engaged to a Spanish goat herder," she announced.

"Gosh, I hadn't realised that you knew him that well," said Robert.

Ali started to laugh but then realised that Robert appeared to be serious; he must know that she was joking, surely.

"Robert's just sold his engineering business and he's taking a break before he decides what to do next." Ronny looked meaningfully at Ali. "And how to spend all his lovely money."

Perhaps a sense of humour's not vital after all, thought Ali. She could laugh herself senseless in a Bentley convertible. She spied Lee and Des and waved them over. The band was starting to play and was really quite good. Ali thought fleetingly how much Jack would have loved it.

They did a few covers of UK and American hits but what really got the audience going were their renditions of Spanish songs. Everyone crowded onto the dancefloor, including Ali, Lee and Ronny, although the men continued to prop up the bar.

When a slower number was played, Robert asked Ali to dance. Both being tall, they looked good together and Ali enjoyed the sensation of being held by a man again.

"You're a very good dancer, Ali," Robert murmured into her ear.

"Yes, well I taught Darcy Bussell everything she knows."

"Really, were you at the Royal Ballet?"

Ali stopped and looked up at Robert's face but, again, she could see no amusement there.

"Oh, yes I see, another joke. I can tell that you have a good sense of humour, like me. Darcy Bussell… ha ha, very good."

Just before Ali decided to leave, Robert asked her if she would have dinner with him the following evening "as we are both on our own". Ali looked furiously at Ronny and Lee, whose innocent expressions confirmed to Ali that they had been talking about her to Robert. Still, it was either warmed up carrot and pepper casserole (not one of her best efforts) or dinner out with an undeniably handsome man – a rich handsome man. He was bound to take her somewhere expensive. She agreed to meet him at the corner bar at 8.30 the next night.

Lee knocked on the door of Casa Lucia the following morning. She said that she was just passing but, as there were no shoe shops at the end of Ali's road, Ali knew that Lee had come to supervise her outfit for tonight. Ali gave in gracefully; actually it was rather nice to have someone to help her.

"Now," said Lee, whisking through Ali's wardrobe, "do you want to say 'let's just be friends'," and she held up a navy linen dress with a high neckline, "or, go all out

with 'I haven't had a shag in months and I'm desperate'?"
She produced a leopard print cat suit that Ali had bought in
Debenhams' sale and never had the nerve to wear.

Most of Ali's clothes lay in a heap on her bed before
they finally decided on narrow cream trousers and a black
silk shirt: "Perfect," said Lee. "Sexy, but not necessarily
available."

Robert was waiting in the bar when Ali arrived. She saw,
to her surprise, that he was sitting at one of the tables
which had been set for dinner. She had assumed that they
would just be having a drink in the bar before moving on
to somewhere more, well, more special.

"I thought we'd eat here," said Robert, rising to kiss
Ali's cheek. "The set menu is really very reasonable. Here,
have a look."

Ali didn't need to see the menu; she'd eaten everything
on it at least five times. However, Robert smelled heavenly
and looked pretty good too, so she smiled and determined
to enjoy herself. She was just about to tell Robert that the
white Rioja was rather good when he asked the waiter for
a bottle of house red.

The evening did improve after that. Ali asked Robert
about the sale of his business and she enjoyed hearing
about the mechanics of the deal. She realised that she was
missing her work and resolved to do more with her days.
She was supposed to be learning Spanish but, apart from
listening to a few CDs and talking to the shopkeepers and
waiters, she hadn't made much progress. Ali promised
herself that she'd find some proper lessons and start as
soon as possible.

"Do you speak Spanish, Robert?" Ali asked.

"A little. I did learn Italian for a while. I thought it
would impress women."

Robert smiled and Ali thought again how handsome he
was.

"I can't imagine that you have too much trouble in that
regard."

"Well, I've had plenty of girlfriends but I've never met that special person. It can get quite lonely sometimes. Even when you're with other people, you can feel alone, you know?"

"It's not all it's cracked up to be," said Ali with a wry smile. "I thought I'd got that special person but it turned out that I wasn't very special to him; not exclusively anyway. He'd been cheating on me, probably for years."

She shook her head: "Oh, listen to us becoming all maudlin. Let's have something extremely naughty for dessert and cheer ourselves up. I'm going to have the 'chocolate puddings'. I do hope that is a literal translation. How about you?"

Robert suggested that they do without coffee and Ali wasn't sure if that was because it wasn't included in the price of the set meal or because he hoped that she'd invite him back to Casa Lucia. Not particularly happy with either of those motives, Ali said firmly that she would like a coffee and she'd have a brandy to go with it.

As they got up to leave, Ali noticed that Robert hadn't left a tip for the waiter and so she surreptitiously slipped a note onto the table. She couldn't imagine having all Robert's money and yet being so mean. She felt quite sorry for him and even sorrier for the "special one" when he found her.

Robert walked Ali back to Casa Lucia and, when he bent down to kiss her cheek, she turned her head and kissed him on the lips. She wanted to make absolutely sure that she wasn't attracted to him. If there was a spark between them, then she may be able to cope with a few Menu Del Dia's; one didn't just turn one's back on tall, rich and handsome.

"And? Was there anything?"

Lee had come round the next morning for a post mortem.

"Nothing. He hadn't expected me to kiss him and the poor man was just getting into his stride when I said that I thought I could hear the dog barking and dashed inside."

"You haven't got a dog," said Lee. They both laughed.

"I know. I'll have to say that it's run away or died or something." Ali paused. "You don't know anyone who gives Spanish lessons, do you, Lee?"

Lee knew everything that went on in the village. "Yes, your neighbour does. Didn't you know? Haven't you noticed people going in and out of her house?"

"Oh, that's it! I just thought she must be the village prostitute and had a particularly eclectic clientele," grinned Ali.

"She is supposed to be very good. Why don't you go round and speak to her now. I've got to get going anyway. Des wants to go to La Cumbre for lunch. Have you heard of it? It's a new hotel up in the mountains. Apparently, Antonio Banderas went to the opening. I met him once; did I tell you, Ali?" Lee grinned. "It was all I could do to stop myself from walking over and licking his face."

Ali agreed with her neighbour, Mary, that she would have an hour's lesson, three times a week.

"We'll see how you get on but maybe you'd also like to join my conversation class," said Mary. "It's all very well learning the verbs and vocabulary but you just have to get out there and speak the language. I get my pupils together with some of the villagers and everyone speaks Spanish for an hour. I pay them, of course, but they love it; they really enjoy correcting the mistakes."

Mary said that she'd see Ali the next day at three and told her to bring an exercise book.

Walking back from the general store with two new exercise books and a set of pens, Ali felt excited and a little apprehensive. It was a long time since she'd done any formal learning. As a solicitor she'd had to attend courses a couple of times a year in order to keep her knowledge up to date but this felt different; it felt like going back to school.

117

CHAPTER TWENTY

Ali didn't often think about her time at university. At first it was because she couldn't bear to and, as the years passed, not looking back had become a habit. She'd been twenty-eight when she finally went, driving to and fro every day, dashing out of lectures as soon as they'd finished to collect Lucy from nursery school. Because Ali didn't socialise with her fellow students, she didn't make any close friendships during her time there. Everyone was pleasant enough but her age and circumstances put her apart. The only exception to this was Ben.

Ali had been a little disappointed to find that the only other mature student on her law degree course was a man. At first Ben was reserved, aloof even, but they often found that they had been paired together for an exercise or case study and, gradually, Ben opened up and Ali enjoyed his company very much.

Ben was thirty and had been a policeman when he'd decided to resign and study law. He'd had to give up his flat and move back in with his parents.

"It's a bit weird living with your Mum and Dad when you're my age," Ben had told Ali. "Mum tends to treat me as though I was still about twelve sometimes but it was good of them to take me in; I couldn't afford to do this otherwise."

Ali found that they worked very well together. Ben had a practical approach, which matched her own and, in their criminal law course, in particular, his experience in the police was really helpful.

"There's no way that I'm becoming a criminal lawyer, though Ali. I don't want to be called out to the station at three in the morning because one of my clients has been caught breaking and entering for the twentieth time. No, I want to work for one of the city firms, doing corporate deals. That's where the money is." Ben grinned. "And I'll wear one of those suits with really broad pinstripes and pink lining."

Ali laughed: "And get some glasses, Ben. I think you can charge more if you wear glasses; the clients will expect it."

During the second term, after the Christmas break, the students were asked to prepare for a mock trial. Ali and Ben had been allocated roles in the defence team and they spent hours in the university library preparing their case. One day, when they'd had an early lecture, Ben asked Ali if she wanted to go back to his parent's house for the rest of the day.

"They're both out at work so we won't be interrupted and we can pace about practicing our speeches without getting told off by the librarians." Ben cocked his head and looked at Ali. "And I expect my Mum will have left some biscuits out for me – chocolate probably."

"Oh well, in that case, what are we waiting for, let's go."

Ben's parent's house was exactly as Ali had imagined. It was a neat 1930's semi with a narrow hallway leading to a front room containing a three-piece suite in cream leather and a large TV set. He led Ali into an immaculate kitchen and offered her coffee.

"It's only instant, I'm afraid. My Dad thinks the real stuff is too bitter."

Ali wanted to see Ben's bedroom. "I do hope you've got a Spiderman duvet, Ben," she said, running up the stairs. "Gosh," she said, stopping at the door to his room. "You're certainly in touch with your feminine side."

The bedroom was decorated entirely in pink; pink bedding, pink carpet, even a pink TV.

"Yes, ha ha. It's my sister's room. They never got around to re-decorating it when she moved out. I don't really notice it any more, to tell you the truth."

"It seems funny being in your parent's house whilst they're out," said Ali. "Let's go and make out on their bed."

She laughed and turned to Ben but, instead of laughing too, he said, "You must know how I feel about you, Ali. I think about you all the time. I think I'm in love with you," and he took a step towards her.

"Ben!" Ali jumped back. "What on earth are you doing? You know I'm married. Is this why you asked me here? Did you think that we would spend the afternoon in bed together?"

Ben held up his hands: "No, no, not at all. I hadn't meant to say anything. Seeing you here, in my home, it just sort of came out. I'm sorry, I know your situation. Look, let's just forget this happened, can we?"

They went downstairs and worked for a while on their speeches for the trial but the atmosphere remained tense and, after an hour, Ali said that she'd better go before the traffic built up. Driving home, she wondered if she had misled Ben into thinking that she wanted a relationship with him. If she was honest with herself, she'd known that Ben found her attractive; she'd seen him looking at her and he often complimented her on what she was wearing or how she'd done her hair.

If she was even more honest with herself, she'd enjoyed his attention and had developed a banter with him that was, at times, undoubtedly flirtatious. And Ben was a good looking man. He was very dark with deep brown, almost black eyes. His hair was starting to recede but he kept it very short and his body was fit and muscular.

However, flirting was one thing but Ali was very happily married to Jack and she had no desire to take it further. She felt angry with Ben for presuming that she did and wondered how they were going to cope in the future, now that he had made his feelings clear.

Ali didn't have to wait long to find out. When she had collected a surprised Lucy from the nursery an hour before her usual time, the phone was ringing as she walked into her house. It was Ben, apologising for his behaviour and asking if they could please just forget it ever happened and go on as before.

For a while they did just that but, increasingly, Ali found herself reliving Ben's words and, when the university broke for the Easter holiday, she missed seeing him every day. They often spoke on the telephone; they had essays to complete and, as they had always done, they shared their research and ideas. Jack had wanted to go to Cornwall for a few days but Ali suggested that he take Lucy whilst she stayed at home, saying that she had too much work to do. That was true but Ali didn't admit to herself that she also wanted to be able to speak to Ben every day.

The final term of the first year went quickly. Much of it was spent reviewing what they had learned and preparing for the end of year exams. On the day of the last exam most of the students on Ali's course were planning on going into town for a pub crawl followed by an Indian meal. They tried to persuade Ali and Ben to join them.

"You never come out drinking with us. Come on, it's the last day of the year."

"We need you with us, Ben. What if we get arrested; you can get your old mates to let us go."

"I've just got to see you pissed at least once, Ali."

Ben said that Ali was welcome to stay the night at his parent's house: "Nothing funny, I promise. Anyway, they'll be there, watching your every move in case you try and nick the porcelain figurines."

When Ali told Jack that she might stay the night at a friend's house and did he mind looking after Lucy, he encouraged her to go: "If your friend doesn't mind you sharing her room, then why not? You go and enjoy yourself."

Ali didn't enlighten him further.

Setting off from home on the last day of term Ali hadn't decided whether or not she would go out drinking and stay at Ben's. Part of her wanted to very much; the part that thought about how Ben's eyes followed her whenever she crossed the room. The other part of her; the part that was a happily married mother of a young girl, knew that she should have one drink and then get in her car and drive home to her family. Yes, that's what she'd do. She put her overnight bag in her car anyway, just in case; she'd almost definitely leave it in the car.

When they got to the fifth pub they played a game with rather obscure rules but which involved Ali kissing Ben firstly on his ear and then on his mouth. The sexual tension which had been building up between them all year was finally released and, having started to kiss, they found they couldn't stop. Luckily, most of the other students were either occupied with the game or too drunk to notice, although one or two did shout: "Hey, look at Ali and Ben" and "About time, you guys."

When everyone decided to move on to a restaurant, Ali and Ben hung back and, waving to a taxi, drove back to Ben's parent's home, oblivious to anything but each other. When they reached the house it was in darkness.

"They'll still be out," said Ben, guiding a rather wobbly Ali inside. "They've gone round to my auntie's."

Ben fetched a bottle of wine and two glasses and they went up to his bedroom, stopping on every stair to kiss. Ali lay on Ben's bed and he lay besides her, stroking her cheek.

"You're so beautiful, Ali. I can't believe you are here with me."

He moved his hand down and slowly ribbed his thumb over her nipple. Ali put her arms around him and felt the muscles running down his back. She pressed herself against him and could feel his hardness. She raised her mouth to his and they kissed more deeply and urgently than before. Ben undid the button on her jeans and Ali lifted up her body so that he could pull them off. As she did so she kicked her handbag, which had been on the bed beside her and it fell to the floor, tumbling its contents onto the carpet. Ali leant down to look and, in the pink glow of the bedside lamp, saw the smiling faces of Lucy and Jack. Her wallet had fallen open and her favourite photograph of her husband and daughter was lying innocently on the floor in front of her eyes.

Ali picked up the photograph and sat on the edge of the bed.

"Is that your family?" Ben sat down next to her and looked down at the photo.

Ali stood up and started to put everything back into her handbag.

"Look, Ben, perhaps this wasn't such a good idea. I'll just leave."

"You can't go now, Ali, you've had far too much to drink. Stay in here. I'll sleep in the spare room. We can talk in the morning. Do you want anything? Something to eat?"

"No, I just want to go to sleep. I'm so sorry, Ben. I should never have started all this. God, what a mess."

"Yes, well, I knew what your situation was didn't I? Is your case still in your car? Do you want me to get it for you?"

Ali's car was parked outside in the drive, where she'd left it earlier.

"No, don't worry about it now." Ali paused and looked at Ben. She could see the disappointment in his face. "I'm sorry," she said again. "I'll see you in the morning."

Ali woke up in the pink bedroom and, for a moment, wondered where she was. When the events of last night came back to her, she groaned. That she'd been very drunk was no excuse. She'd behaved so badly. Not only had she very nearly cheated on her husband, she'd led Ben on, knowing how he felt about her. She'd loved how he'd made her feel and now their friendship was ruined and it was all her fault.

The house was quiet and Ali gathered her things and crept downstairs. She left a note on the kitchen table saying that she'd had to leave early and thanking them for putting her up. She'd call Ben later; she couldn't face him now. She got in her car and drove, very carefully and with an aching head, back home.

Opening the front door, Ali could hear Jack and Lucy in the kitchen. Lucy was giggling and, as she walked in, she saw that Jack was making pancakes with Lucy's help.

"Mummy! I've made pancakes. Well, Daddy helped a bit but I did the stirring. That's the importantest part you see."

"Hello, darling. Sorry about the mess. Did you have fun?"

They both seemed so pleased to see her that Ali had to turn away so that they wouldn't see her guilty tears.

A week later Ben called Ali and asked if she'd meet him near the university for a coffee. The course was finished for the summer and she hadn't seen or spoken to Ben since the night at his parent's. She hadn't called him; she knew that she should but she hadn't been able to think what to say.

She'd thought about him a lot and knew that it wasn't just the drink that had made her behave as she had. She realised that she had quite strong feelings for him and in different circumstances she'd have had a relationship with him, maybe something lasting but her life was with her husband and daughter. It was almost as though what happened at university wasn't real; she was a different person there and Ali recognised the danger of that.

Driving to meet Ben, Ali wondered what she was going to say. She supposed that he would try to persuade her to leave Jack and be with him and she rehearsed in her mind how she would gently let him know that that was not going to happen.

"So, that's it really, Ali. I'm setting off in a couple of weeks and I expect to be away for at least a year, if I ever come back, that is."

Ben had told Ali that he couldn't bear to stay around, seeing her every day at the university, loving and wanting her but knowing that she was in love with someone else and that they'd never be together.

"I knew, seeing your face when you looked at the photo

of your husband and daughter, that it wasn't going to happen with us. I'm glad what happened that night actually because it made me see things more clearly. I'd never really thought properly about your other life before now.

"So I'm going to travel. I've got relatives in Sydney and I'm starting there and after that, I'll just see how it goes. I've got no ties, after all."

"But what about your degree, Ben? You'll have wasted a whole year."

"Oh, I'm not really sure that being stuck in an office all day is for me, Ali. I'd rather be out, doing things. Anyway, the year wasn't wasted; I met you."

They looked at one another. "I'm so sorry, Ben, if I led you on at all."

"You didn't, Ali. Well, apart from last week when you threw yourself at me shamelessly." Ben smiled and then looked serious. "If I'd met you first, do you think we'd have made a go of it?"

Ali reached for his hand: "I've been thinking about that driving up here and, yes, I think we would have." She looked into his eyes: "You'll make some girl a wonderful husband. I feel quite jealous already. Will you keep in touch and let me know how you're getting on?"

Ali realised suddenly just how much she was going to miss him. If only she hadn't allowed matters to come to a head then they could have carried on just being good friends. But, as soon as she thought this she knew that it wasn't true; something was bound to happen between them sooner or later.

"I feel that the only way I can do this, Ali, is if we don't contact each other at all. But I will always be thinking of you, you should know that."

Ben stood up: "Let's not prolong this. I'm just going to leave now. Goodbye, my lovely girl," and he walked out.

Ali never heard from him again.

CHAPTER TWENTY-ONE

Lee had raved about the lunch she'd had at La Cumbre and so when Robert asked her if she'd like to go there for dinner on Saturday night Ali said yes. She'd been feeling a bit low. Paul was still away in Granada and she'd spent too many evenings on her own or sitting in the local bars with other couples. It would be nice to be the centre of someone's attention for once.

The hotel was an hour's drive from Compesita and, noting that Robert drove very well, Ali relaxed and enjoyed the view. She'd never been this far North of the village and the scenery was spectacular. The road wound upwards past Almond orchards which would look wonderful when the blossom was out. Eventually, they came to the brow of a hill and Robert turned the car into a gravel driveway. The hotel was in what had clearly once been an old farmhouse and, although the exterior was neatly painted and Bougainvillea clung prettily to its iron shutters, it looked homely rather than grand. Once inside, however, Ali could see why Lee had been so enthusiastic. The interior, which had presumably been a series of small dark rooms, had been completely opened out to make one large room with picture windows at the far end through which the Almond orchards curved gently into the distance. Everything was white; the walls, the floor and the furniture and abstract paintings hung on each wall.

Ali turned to Robert and smiled, "What an amazing place, Robert. I'm so pleased that you brought me here."

As there were quite a few diners seated already, they elected to go straight to their table and Ali was delighted when they were seated in front of the window. The hotel manager had greeted them and led them to their table; he seemed to know Robert well and Ali wondered how many other women he'd brought here for dinner and if her first meal with him at the local bar had been some sort of test. Well, if it was, she'd clearly passed it and the thought made her smile.

"What's amused you, Ali? It certainly can't be these prices. I'm sure they've put them up since I was last here."

"Have you been many times before?" asked Ali. "I thought that they hadn't been open very long."

"No, only a few months but it's the only decent place for miles. Now, I can recommend the lamb."

Because she thought that he'd enjoy it, Ali asked Robert to choose for her and she sat back to observe the other diners. There was an elderly lady with whom Ali assumed was her son. *Oh, my goodness, not her son then*, thought Ali, seeing the old lady place a bejewelled hand on the young man's thigh and give it a squeeze.

On another table were a couple, both beautiful and completely enraptured with one another. The woman had very long dark blonde hair done in a high pony tail, which hung down her tanned back. Noticing how upright the woman held herself, Ali straightened her own shoulders and turned her attention to Robert. One or two of the other diners were looking at them and Ali thought that she and Robert made quite a handsome couple themselves.

The food Robert had chosen for them was perfect; grilled asparagus followed by lamb. The wine, too, was very good, although he'd ordered only half bottles; one each of white and red. She remembered her friend Carolyn once telling her that she'd ended a promising relationship with a man because he'd sent her half a bottle of Champagne on her birthday.

"I mean honestly, Ali," she'd said, "imagine going to the trouble of ordering wine to be delivered and then asking for half a bottle. He had to go straight away."

However, Ali excused Robert; he was driving after all.

During their main course a table of four close to them had become increasingly loud and annoying. One of the men, in particular, appeared to have had too much to drink and he now started shouting rudely at the waiter,

"Hey you, over here. What's this muck? I'm not eating this, it's raw."

The manager rushed over and tried to calm things down but the man, egged on by his plump wife, only became more irate.

"At the prices you charge we expect better than this. I've had better beef at our local carvery."

The manager, whilst remaining polite, told the four that, if they were not satisfied, then he would waive the bill and no doubt they would prefer to leave straight away. In the silence that followed their huffing departure, Ali found herself desperately missing Jack. Instead of looking embarrassed and uncomfortable, as Robert did now, Jack would have seen that Ali was upset by the other table's rudeness and distracted her by telling jokes; either that or he'd have gone over and told the man to shut up.

Shortly after Robert had given the waiter his credit card, the manager came to their table and asked Robert to follow him. Ali hoped that there wasn't a problem with Robert's card. The 50€ she had in her purse probably wouldn't pay for the asparagus, let alone the whole bill.

When he came back Robert looked angry, "That damned man on the next table, the one who made all the fuss, has only backed his car into mine. There's not a lot of damage luckily but the front wheel's buckled. We can't drive it tonight. We'll have to stay here."

Ali's first thought was that this was all part of an elaborate plot to make her spend the night with him but, when she saw how upset he was, she changed her mind. However, she said firmly, "Do they have two rooms available?"

"What? Oh yes, of course. The manager was terribly apologetic and they are preparing two of their best rooms straight away. Apparently one of the waiters has a brother with a garage and he'll come over in the morning with a new tyre."

Ali slept well in an extremely comfortable bed. She rang down for her breakfast to be delivered to her room, not wanting to sit in the dining room in last night's clothes.

She was just finishing her coffee when Robert knocked on her door: "Hi, Ali, may I come in?"

He too was looking refreshed and cheerful, although he had bad news about his car. "It seems that they have to order a new wheel and that will take goodness knows how long. Anyway, the garage is lending me a car. I think this must be it arriving now."

He and Ali went to the window and watched as a sleek Audi TT pulled into the gravel drive.

On the drive home Ali turned to Robert and said, "You should have seen your face when the garage chap led us straight past the Audi and handed you the keys to this old banger. You have to admit, it was quite funny."

Robert's mouth gave a twitch, "But it's so damned uncomfortable, Ali. My knees are wedged right under the steering wheel. God knows how I'll get out. And it's orange, for heaven's sake. Who on earth would want an orange car."

"Well, to be fair, not completely orange, Robert. The rear wing's purple, I think you'll find."

Ali couldn't stop laughing and eventually Robert joined in and the journey back to Compesita in the rattling old Seat Ibiza turned out to be rather fun.

Jack was finding life without Ali hard. He was used to being on his own during the week but, when he returned to the cottage on Friday evenings, he dreaded the weekend ahead of him. Often, rather than eat a microwaved meal for one in the solitary kitchen, he walked down to The Feathers only to become depressed by the smiling couples, or worse, single men like himself, nursing halves of bitter, pathetically glad of a few words from the barmaid.

He spent much of his time at his golf club but, after the game, his partners usually downed a quick pint and then dashed home to their wives and children, leaving Jack to return alone to face a long afternoon with the Sunday papers and his regrets. He'd joined a gym but could rarely summon the enthusiasm to go.

He had gone out for dinner with a woman he'd met at a conference but, although she was attractive and seemingly keen on him, he kept comparing her unfavourably with Ali. Without realising it, he must have spoken of her often during the meal because, at the end of the evening, the woman had thanked him for dinner and suggested that he call her when he'd got over his wife. It was ironic that, having as much freedom as he wished to date and sleep with other women, he found that he didn't want to. What he wanted was to have his wife back.

Ali was struggling with her Spanish homework when she got a call from Paul to say he was back from his trip to Granada and was she free to meet for a drink that evening. She found that she was really looking forward to seeing him again and dressed carefully in narrow jeans and a green cashmere jumper that Emma had bought her one Christmas and which matched her eyes.

She was a little early but decided to walk up to the bar and wait for Paul. It was a beautiful evening and Ali sat on the terrace, watching the villagers come and go across the square. When Paul arrived it was obvious that he was pleased to see her too. Giving her a long hug and smiling into her eyes he said, "I've missed you, Ali. You look amazing. Is that cashmere?" He ran his fingers up her arm.

Ali laughed: "For a straight man you certainly know your fabrics."

"I'm a very tactile person, Ali," Paul said, still stroking her sleeve. "I hate anything itchy against my skin. My mother was a great knitter. You name it, she knitted it. Everything I wore up to the age of twelve was made out of wool. It was really embarrassing when I went swimming."

They shared a bottle of Rioja and Paul told Ali of his stay in Granada.

"It's an amazing place. The Alhambra is wonderful, of course, but what I really love to do is just wander about and get lost. You see so much that way."

He told Ali that part of the reason for his trip was to research for a book he was writing about the Spanish Civil War.

"It's such a fascinating period, Ali. You wouldn't believe the hardships that the ordinary people had to endure."

As the evening wore on Ali realised how much she'd missed Paul when he'd been away. He was always such good company. He never dominated the conversation and seemed genuinely interested in other people. She also found him very attractive and thought with a thrill of anticipation that he appeared to like her too. When Ali said that she'd never been to Granada Paul suggested that she accompany him on his next visit.

"I'll certainly be going back in a month or so. I've found this lovely little hotel. It's not at all expensive but it has a wonderful terrace on the roof and the food is fantastic."

Ali was just about to tell Paul about her eventful stay at La Cumbre when they were interrupted by Robert: "Ali darling, how are you? Mind if I join you?"

"Oh. Hi, Robert, err no, not at all. Do you know Paul?"

The two men nodded to each other, rather curtly thought Ali, wanting to laugh.

"I'm glad I ran into you actually, Ali. The hotel rang. Apparently, you left one of your earrings in the bedroom when we stayed last week. I can pick it up for you when I go back for the car."

Robert turned to Paul and started to tell him about the problem with his car but Ali could see that Paul wasn't really listening and, after a while, he stood up and said coolly, "Well, I'll leave you two together. You've clearly got a lot to talk about."

As he turned to walk away, Ali could see the hurt and disappointment in his eyes.

"Oh don't go, Paul. Stay and have another drink. We haven't finished the bottle yet."

"I'm sure that Richard, wasn't it, can help you with

that. Although I expect that it's not up to the same standard as the hotels you frequent. Here," Paul put some money on the table, "that should cover it. Goodnight."

And he walked stiffly away.

As quickly as she could after that, Ali made her excuses and left, brushing aside Robert's offer to walk her home. Back in Casa Lucia, she got ready for bed and thought about her evening. It was obvious that Paul had jumped to the conclusion that she and Robert had spent the night together in La Cumbre. What surprised her a little was how much that had appeared to upset Paul. She was even more surprised at how much she wanted Paul to know that she hadn't slept with Robert and never would.

She decided to go and see Paul in the morning and clear things up. First though, she'd call on Robert and tell him that, although she enjoyed his company, she really wasn't ready to take their relationship any further.

When Ali walked over to Ronny and Alan's house early the following morning, she found Robert sitting in the garden reading.

"Ali, how lovely. Ronny and Alan are both out, I'm afraid. You'll have to do with just me."

"It was you I came to see actually, Robert. The thing is…"

Robert interrupted her, "Here, have some of this Lemonade. Ronny made it. I think she puts ginger in or something. It's certainly delicious."

Robert poured her a glass.

"Thank you. Well, Robert, you see I really enjoy your company and, oh, what is it?"

Robert had jumped up and was waving his arms around.

"Nothing, just a wasp. Blasted things. Now then, Ali. Actually, before you go on, there is something that I wanted to say myself. I know we've had some lovely times together, really super, but I've been talking to Ronny and she said that it's only fair that I make my feelings clear.

"I hope that you won't be too upset, Ali, although I do have a handkerchief with me just in case, ha ha, but I don't think that we are really compatible. I mean, you are a marvellous girl but there's just something missing for me and I felt that I should tell you before you got too hurt."

"Oh, I see. Well, thank you for being so honest, Robert."

"You're not too devastated?"

"I think I'll get over it. Oh look, there's that wasp again. Has it stung you, Robert? Oh dear, you poor thing."

CHAPTER TWENTY-TWO

The following Friday Ali drove to the airport and boarded an early morning flight to the UK. It was Simon and Cici's wedding the next day and she'd promised Emma that she would be there to support her. The reception was to be held at Cici's parent's farmhouse in North Devon with a service beforehand in the village church. Although Ali was worried about how her friend would cope with the wedding, Ali was looking forward to spending a few days back in England.

Mindful of her budget, Ali had decided against buying a new outfit and planned to make do with a dress and hat she had bought the year before for a trip to Ascot. It would be perfect for a country wedding and she planned to call into her cottage and pick it up. She'd phoned Jack to ask if he minded her dropping by and he'd sounded pathetically grateful to hear from her. Ali had stressed that it would just be a fleeting visit and she'd arranged to spend the night with Linda and Carl in London before driving to Devon early the next day.

Before going to her old home, Ali was meeting her client John Drake. He'd called her a couple of weeks ago and said that there was something he'd like to discuss with her. He told her that he was back in England, he'd had enough of travelling. Ali wondered what he wanted although she wasn't surprised to hear of his return; he wasn't the sort of man who could be idle for long.

Ali collected a rental car at the airport and drove to John's house, which was en route to her cottage. Both John and his wife greeted her warmly and John told her in his usual forthright manner,

"I was bored fartless, Ali; not enough to do, that was the trouble. You can only visit so many sodding chateaus. I'm going to get back into the property game but this time I'm going to buy existing buildings, do 'em up and rent 'em out.

"I'm planning on a mix of residential and commercial, starting with student lets. There's money to be made there, I'm bloody sure of it."

He put down his coffee cup and looked at Ali, "I'd like you to join me. Come and work for me and deal with all the legal bumph. It might not be full time, not straight off anyway, but I'll pay you well and you can base yourself wherever you like. You can stay in blinking Spain if you want. What d'you say?"

Ali told John that she'd think it over and let him know. In the meantime, he promised to send her his business plan and projections for the first five years. As she left he gave her a hug, "You're looking good, girl. Whatever you've been up to in that Costa Del Crime it fucking suits you."

Ali pulled up outside her cottage. It looked so familiar. She felt instantly as though she'd never been away and was returning home after a normal Friday at the office. She realised just how happy she'd been in her old life, the life she'd had before Jack ruined everything.

Her feeling of nostalgia continued when she walked into the hall and could see Jack in the kitchen. The lamps were lit and jazz was playing in the background. Jack had his back to her and was tasting something on the stove. Ali couldn't stop herself from smiling when she heard him say "not bad, old boy".

She put her case down and said softly, "Hello, Jack."

He turned round and Ali could see his handsome face and the breadth of his shoulders; the manliness of him.

"Hello you. I hope you don't mind me being here. I wasn't sure if you wanted to see me or not." He paused and smiled at her: "You're looking lovely, Ali. I like your hair that way."

Jack poured her a drink and, as she sat at the kitchen table, Ali could see what trouble he'd gone to. As well as the delicious smell of the meal he was cooking, the place was spotlessly clean and there were flowers on the dresser.

"I didn't know what time you'd arrive or if you'd have

eaten but I thought I'd have something ready, just in case. It's only pasta with a red pepper sauce but…"

Ali interrupted him: "It all sounds great, Jack, thank you. And the house looks good."

Jack smiled: "I expect you thought I'd be an unshaven mess, living on cat food and whiskey. I've quite enjoyed cooking for myself, well it's given me something to do."

Ali went upstairs to find her wedding outfit. Their bedroom, too, was neat and tidy and she was touched to see that Jack had put a photograph of her and Lucy next to his bed. Going over to take a closer look she saw that he was reading one of her favourite novels. In happier times she'd have enjoyed discussing it with him.

Jack called up the stairs to say that the meal was ready and Ali sat opposite him in the kitchen, as she had done so many times in the past. They talked about Lucy and of Jack's work and Ali told him about her efforts to learn Spanish. Once or twice Ali almost forgot about the past few months and it was as though she'd never been away. When it grew dark Ali stood up and said that she must be going as Linda was expecting her.

Jack stood up too and cleared his throat before saying, "Before you leave, Ali, I must say what's on my mind. I've missed you so badly and, seeing you here tonight, having you back in our home, has made me realise just how much. Life without you is meaningless for me. I just exist. I go to work, I play golf, I see friends but none of it has any joy for me anymore.

"I can't let you go tonight without asking you, begging you even, for one last chance. I'd do anything, go anywhere if it meant that I could be with you. I'm just no good without you."

Jack's voice broke and he breathed deeply, squeezing his eyes shut.

Ali was moved by his words and his obvious distress and she walked over and put her arms around him. Suddenly, they were kissing and, in between kisses, Jack murmured endearments into her ear. It felt good, it felt right to be in his arms and, when Jack put his hand on her back and guided her upstairs, lay her on the bed and made love to her, it was where she wanted to be. They both woke in the night to make love again. Their bodies were so familiar to one another, each knew the other's desires.

In the morning Ali had to set off early for the drive to Devon and she untangled herself from Jack's sleepy embrace, dressed quickly and silently left. She wrote a note saying that she'd come back on Sunday afternoon and they could talk then and left it on the kitchen table where Jack would see it when he came down. As Ali put her bag in the car her phone rang and, seeing it was Linda, she cut it off. She didn't want to speak to her sister until she'd had time to gather her thoughts. She'd sent her a brief text at some point last night to say that something had cropped up and she wouldn't be staying that night. Knowing her sister, she'd be full of curiosity about what had happened.

Driving through the quiet lanes in the early morning sunlight, Ali felt wonderful. It must be the sex, she thought, releasing all those marvellous hormones into her bloodstream and she relived again and again the previous night in bed with Jack. It wasn't just the love making itself, it was the intimacy. Having someone stroke your face and kiss you and, afterwards, to lie with your head on someone's chest and feel their heart beating.

And Jack really did love her so much. He'd cried again after they'd made love for the first time and had said such sweet things to her that she'd found herself telling him that she loved him too, that she'd never stopped loving him.

By the time she'd reached the M5, Ali's euphoria had lessened slightly and she allowed other thoughts and other people to enter her head. Emma, whom she would see in just a few hours, would be horrified to learn that she'd slept with Jack and was thinking of going back to him. If, indeed, that was what she wanted. Ali suddenly went cold when she reminded herself that the man who last night adored her had also lied and cheated. Was it possible that

Jack could ever change? Was she being unbelievably stupid to even consider that he would be faithful to her? She decided to just allow her feelings to settle down and to see how she felt after the wedding. She'd trust her instincts; they didn't often let her down.

Ali made good progress and arrived at the pub where she and Emma had booked rooms for the night by mid-morning. The ceremony wasn't until three and so she had plenty of time to get ready. Her room was still being cleaned and so Ali ordered a late breakfast and went through into the dining room. She was absolutely starving.

"And what are you looking so pleased with yourself about, Madam?" Emma walked into the dining room and gave Ali a hug. "You must have set off even earlier than me. Wasn't the M25 a bugger, even at that time in the morning?"

Ali made non-committal noises. She didn't want to tell Emma that she hadn't spent the night in Linda's spare room in North London but in Jack's bed.

Their rooms were ready and they went upstairs. The pub was an old coaching inn with sloping floors and dark panelled walls. Their bedrooms both overlooked the rear courtyard and were spacious and pretty, in a rather floral way. As the two rooms were adjoining and had a connecting door, they asked the landlady if it could be opened and she stamped off rather crossly to find the key.

"I expect she thinks that we are lovers and thinks we will frighten the horses or something," whispered Ali.

They went into Emma's room and while they waited for the landlady to return, Ali hid her dismay when she saw her friend's suit, which, as the best woman, she was to wear with a pink shirt and a grey and pink cravat. How much less of a cliché it would have been if Emma had worn a pretty, flouncy dress.

"A woman from the hairdressers in the next village is coming over to put my hair up," said Emma.

"I nearly refused on the basis that the salon is called From Hair To Eternity. Isn't that dreadful? But apparently it's either that or Madame Helena, which is run by the butcher's wife. Although I'm told she does do a very good bacon barmcake, whatever that is. I expect the local salon will put it up into a beehive. Actually, that might be quite cool."

Emma held her long blonde hair above her head and twirled in front of the mirror.

"What are you wearing, Als?"

"I'll show you in a bit. It's that Ted Baker dress I wore to Ascot last year, remember? The navy one with green and yellow flowers. I've brought two hats. I need you to tell me which one looks less ghastly."

"So did you go back to the cottage to pick up your dress? Did you see Casanova?"

"I did see Jack, yes." *Actually*, thought Ali, *I saw a little more of him than I expected to.* "Anyway, let's not talk about him. How do you feel now that the big day has arrived?"

They were interrupted by the landlady bringing the door key and they risked incurring her further wrath by deciding it would be a very good idea to have a glass of Champagne.

"Oh, we don't sell it by the glass, dear. I can let you have a bottle if you like. I'll send George up with it."

The friends, assuming that George was the landlady's husband and expecting someone red faced and wheezy, were delighted when an extremely handsome young man knocked on their door and entered blushingly with a bottle of Moet and Chandon and two glasses.

"You ladies here for the wedding then?"

When they said that they were he shyly said that he was helping out at the reception and so he might see them later. After he'd left, gratefully pocketing Emma's ten pound tip, she grinned at Ali.

"I'm so going to snog him tonight. Actually, I'll probably bring him back to my room so we'd better re-lock the connecting door. I don't want you luring him away with your tanned legs and sun bleached curls.

139

Seriously though Ali, you look really good at the mo. I don't know what you've been up to in Spain but it certainly suits you."

Emma wanted to have a nap before the hairdresser arrived and so Ali went into her room and had a shower. Looking at her phone she saw that she'd received a text from Jack:

'I hope you arrived safely, darling. I keep thinking of last night. I can't wait to see you tomorrow.' xxx

Ali wasn't sure how to reply, her mind was still uncertain, so she just texted:

'We'll talk tomorrow,' and, after hesitating, added one kiss. There was a whole wealth of meaning in text kisses.

At two o'clock Ali put on her Ted Baker dress and reached into her case for her shoes. To her horror she realised that, in her haste to pack, she'd brought one black shoe and one navy one. She padded down the corridor to the bar in her stockings to look for the landlady.

"Hello? Hello? Oh, yes, hi, I don't suppose there is a shoe shop in the village is there? You won't believe it but I've brought odd shoes."

"No, dear, there's the newsagents and the baker but that's it. You'd have to go into Tiverton for shoes and that's a good thirty minutes away."

Ali's face fell. She'd just have to wear the old flat sandals she wore for driving. The landlady glanced down at Ali's feet.

"What size are you, dearie? I could lend you a pair of mine. I take a three but a seven's more comfortable." The landlady broke into wheezy laughter.

Although they were the same size Ali wondered briefly whether to lie. She didn't like the thought of wearing someone else's shoes and God only knew what hideous monstrosities this woman would possess.

Ali met Emma in the bar at half past two so they could walk to the church together. Despite Ali's initial doubts, Emma looked enchanting in her tiny man's suit. Her blonde hair shone in a French pleat and she looked composed and determined.

"I've decided to enjoy today, Ali. And, starting tomorrow, I'm going to move on with my life. You know, I spent last evening with Simon, holding his hand as he got more and more drunk. I listened to him telling me just how much he loved another woman and I thought to myself, this is madness, my obsession with him has got to stop.

"This time next year you'll be attending my wedding, just you see," Emma paused. "Wow, Ali, I love your shoes. Where did you find those?"

Ali laughed: "Come on I'll tell you on the way. We don't want to be late."

The landlady's shoe collection had been a revelation. Box after box of designer shoes were stacked in her wardrobe and Ali had no difficulty finding a pair to match her outfit.

"Are you sure you don't mind lending them to me? They look brand new and they must have cost a fortune."

"Not at all, dear. Shoes are my little luxury but I hardly ever go anywhere to wear them. I'll enjoy thinking of you dancing the night away in this pair. That's what they were made for."

The wedding was perfect. The old church had been decorated with wild flowers and was packed with well-dressed guests. Cici looked absolutely beautiful in a very simple ivory satin dress with a long veil held by a diamante headband. There were two little bridesmaids and a page boy, who was later found to have scowled fiercely in every photograph. Simon seemed nervous but spoke his part well and there was no doubting the love and pride on his face when he saw his bride for the first time coming down the aisle on her father's arm.

Ali cried, as she always did at weddings and, watching the elderly couple next to her holding hands, she thought of Jack. Was it possible that they would be together and still in love when they were seventy? A couple of days ago she would have said definitely not but now she allowed herself to hope that it may be so.

At the reception, which was held in a marquee in the garden of Cici's parents' rather grand farmhouse, Ali was sat next to a man of about her own age. From his broad shoulders and ruddy cheeks Ali guessed correctly that he was a farmer, like most of Cici's relations. Ali tried desperately to think of something she knew about farming and which might interest him but, to her delight, he started telling her about a book he was reading and they spent most of the first course discussing their favourite authors.

The man, Jim, told her that he was gay but that his mother was still hoping he'd get over it and settle down with a nice girl.

"I do have a boyfriend who runs a restaurant in Tiverton but it's still very traditional here and I just didn't think I could bring him as my partner to Cici's wedding. Everyone knows about Andrew and me but it's not really talked about."

Jim got out his phone and showed Ali a photo of himself with his arm around the shoulders of a good looking man, with dark, closely cropped hair and almond shaped hazel eyes.

"Wow, he's gorgeous," said Ali. Lucky you."

"How about you, Ali? You've come with Emma haven't you? Are you two together?"

"Oh no, we're just friends," Ali laughed. "My situation is a bit complicated, I'm afraid," and, as the waitresses served them with rare roast beef and dauphinoise potatoes, Ali found herself telling Jim everything that had happened between her and Jack.

"So, as you can imagine, I'm in a quandary at the moment." She put her knife and fork down and turned to look at Jim. "Do you think that people can change?"

Jim looked at her hopeful face and said, "Go with your heart, Ali. Don't worry about what other people will say. I should know that trying to please others doesn't make you happy. Sometimes you just have to take a risk. It might not work out but you'll never know if you don't try."

"When I first met Andrew I wasn't sure if he was gay or not. I just knew that I fancied him like mad. I kept going to his restaurant. I was putting on so much weight I was becoming a right fatty bum- bum. Anyway, one evening I walked in and went straight over to him and asked if he'd like to go and see a film. He asked me what was on and I realised that I didn't know; I'd just said the first thing that came into my head. But I tell you, Ali, I'm so so glad that I took the chance."

After the speeches, during which Emma spoke wittily of Simon and movingly of his love for Cici which, Ali knew, must have cost her dearly, the lights in the marquee were dimmed and she dragged a reluctant Jim onto the dancefloor.

"Phew, I'm whacked. These country boys certainly have a lot of energy."

Emma, jacketless and with her cravat tied around her waist, sat down heavily at Ali's table.

"What is it with weddings? I've had two proposals of marriage. I'm trying to decide between Simon's uncle Peter, who assures me that he can still perform what he calls 'the business' and a rather sweet chap who has the farm adjoining Cici's father. Apparently, I'm to have my own frock allowance and the shops around here are smarter than you'd think. There's one not far away where Camilla once bought a cardigan. And his favourite pig is called Emma, so it's practically a done deal.

"He does have rather odd teeth but I've persuaded him to grow a moustache. I don't think you'll notice them so much then. Oh, look, there's gorgeous George. George, woo hoo. Bring me another vod will you, darling. Don't bother with the tonic."

Ali slipped away just after midnight. The band was playing slow, sexy songs and couples were swaying closely together. Emma was being guided rather expertly around the floor by a dapper buck toothed man and seemed happy enough and Ali wanted to be on her own for a while.

Back in her hotel room she removed the landlady's shoes and placed them carefully back in their box. She sat down to send a text to Jack. It just said 'I love you'.

Jack couldn't wait for Sunday afternoon to arrive when he'd see Ali again. He put clean sheets on the bed, washed his car and read the papers but it was still only 11.30 on Saturday morning. In the afternoon he played golf and then watched TV while he ate his dinner. By early evening he was bored and restless and decided to go for a drive and perhaps a drink in town. There was a new wine bar that he thought he could take Ali to, if there was an Ali to take out again. He dearly hoped that there might be.

He noticed her straightaway. She was sat at the bar and she kept looking at her watch. Several times she got out her phone and checked that too. Her heart shaped face was surrounded by a mass of ash blonde corkscrew curls and she had large dark brown eyes, a tiny turned up nose and wide full lips. She was the most beautiful woman that Jack had ever seen. His eyes dropped down and took in her body; slim but curvaceous in a black jersey dress and high heeled boots. He couldn't stop staring at her.

Eventually, he walked over and asked if he could buy her a drink. She looked up at him and smiled. She had small white teeth like a child.

"Why not. It looks as though I've been stood up. I was just about to leave but, thank you, I'll have another Prosecco."

She told him that her name was Charlie and that she worked for an airline. She tossed her hair prettily and said, "I was supposed to meet a guy here that I met on a flight last week. I obviously didn't make a very good first impression."

Jack silently thanked the unknown man, deluded though he clearly was. "I find that very hard to believe. If I had a date with you wild horses couldn't keep me away."

Charlie raised an eyebrow, "Are you flirting with me, Jack? I think I like it."

They had another round of drinks and, when Charlie went to the ladies, Jack looked at his reflection in the mirrored bar and asked himself what he was doing. An hour ago he was full of anticipation about seeing Ali again and now he was chatting up another woman. He stood up to leave just as Charlie came back.

"Leaving already? Your place or mine?" She ran her hand up his leg and stroked his bottom. She had redone her lipstick in the ladies and she looked up at him with parted shiny lips. Jack wondered what it would be like to kiss them. He knew that he probably could if he wanted to and the thought made him feel powerful and more alive than he had in months.

"My place isn't far. Come on, my car's outside."

He started taking her dress off as soon as they'd closed the front door. She was kissing him with a fierceness which excited him intensely and, when he pushed her down onto the stairs and thrust into her, she shivered and uttered strange wild cries.

Later she lay on top of him, completely at ease with her naked body. She started to caress him again, bending down to kiss and lick his chest, her soft curls tickling his stomach.

Jack's phone beeped when she was making them an omelette, wearing nothing but his shirt. She turned to look at him sharply and he switched it off without looking at who the message was from.

They made love all night. Jack had never before known such an inventive and enthusiastic lover. He finally fell asleep at dawn and awoke to find Charlie looking through Ali's wardrobe.

"You and your wife are separated, right? I mean, why has she left so many clothes at your house?"

She came over and sat astride his chest. Her full breasts rose and fell with her breathing and she bent down and

145

kissed him slowly, pushing her tongue deep into his mouth.

"If you want this, Jack, if you want to do this again then it has to be exclusive. I'm not the sort of woman who can share her man."

Jack grabbed her hair and turned her over. He looked down at her perfect body and could see the desire in her half-closed eyes. He did want it. He wanted it more than he'd ever wanted anything.

CHAPTER TWENTY-THREE

Ali woke up early on Sunday morning. She'd heard Emma going into her room at four in the morning and knew that she wouldn't be up for hours and so Ali decided to leave straight away. With any luck the traffic would be light and she'd be back at the cottage by midday. Having made up her mind to give her marriage another try she couldn't wait to see Jack's face when she told him. She wrote a note for Emma and left it with the landlady, thanking her again for the loan of her shoes and promising her that she'd be the first person she'd turn to if she ever had another wardrobe malfunction.

As she drove towards her home Ali imagined Jack's reaction when he heard of her decision. How happy he'd be. Perhaps they could go away together for a few days; she could easily change her flight back to Spain. Or, maybe they'd just stay at the cottage and spend long lazy afternoons curled up in each other's arms. Both Emma and Linda would think she was mad to go back to him but Lucy would be pleased to have her parents together again.

Reaching the cottage, she left her bags in the car and walked quickly up the path. As she opened the front door with her key she heard Jack shout from the kitchen, "Back already? Are you insatiable woman? Come here, you gorgeous thing you."

Ali didn't notice the look of alarm on his face as she laughingly ran into his arms, "I got here as quickly as I could. Have you been missing me that much, you naughty man?"

"Oh, Ali, it's you. I wasn't expecting you so early."

"I know. I couldn't sleep and so I just got in the car and drove back. I haven't even had breakfast." She put her hands on his chest and smiled into his eyes, "I've got something to tell you."

"OK, well, before you do, I've left the shower running upstairs. Just give me a minute. You make some coffee and I'll be right down."

Jack squeezed her hand briefly and walked out of the kitchen.

Ali sat down at the table and looked around at the familiar room. It was lovely to be back in her own home again. She jumped up and reached for the coffee.

"Jack," she called up the stairs, "did you have the boys round? It's a right mess in here."

Ali began to load plates and glasses into the dishwasher, humming to herself. She made some toast and drank her coffee and then began to wonder what was taking Jack so long. She grinned to herself; maybe he's expecting me to join him in the shower. Going into their bedroom she saw that Jack was sitting on the bed with his head bowed.

"What's the matter, darling? Did you have a lot to drink last night? Does your head hurt?"

She sat down on the bed next to him.

"Well, listen, this will make you feel better. I've given this a lot of thought and I think we should try again. You love me and I love you and that's not something we should just throw away. I'm not saying that it will be easy for me but, if we both want to, we can make it work."

Ali looked at her husband expectantly. He sighed and walked over to the window. Turning round to look at her he said, "I don't think we should rush into this, Ali. I think it will be best if you go back to Spain as planned, stay for the full six months and we'll see how we feel then."

Ali smiled and shook her head, "No, you're not listening to me Jack. I know how I feel. I want to come home. I want us to be together again. I've missed you. I've missed us."

She took a step towards him but he held out his hands to stop her.

"I'm sorry but I don't know if that is what I want. I know what I said to you on Friday but I've been thinking about it over the weekend and now I'm not so sure any more."

The realisation of what Jack was saying hit Ali at last and disbelief led to dismay and finally to anger.

"You're not sure? You're not fucking sure? You absolute bastard. I've spent the weekend going over and over what you said to me on Friday. Searching my heart to see if I can forgive you and trust you again. Now, when I come to you and tell you that I want our marriage to work, you tell me that you've changed your mind."

Ali sank back onto the bed.

"Why did you tell me that you loved me; that you couldn't live without me? Why did you make love to me? I was getting my life back together. I was getting over you and you worm your way back into my heart only to push me away. How could you be so cruel Jack?"

Ali gazed at her husband in disgust and slowly stood up.

I must have been out of my mind to have even considered giving you another chance. Well, never again. You can be absolutely sure of that."

Ali turned and stumbled blindly down the stairs. Grabbing her car keys she ran out of the front door and drove away. Hurt and self-pity overcame her and angry tears ran down her face. Her hands were shaking so much on the wheel that she had to pull over and she sat at the side of the road until she could control her breathing.

She got lost several times on the journey to Linda's but eventually she turned into her road and, thankfully finding somewhere to park, she dragged her case to her sister's door. Linda, seeing Ali's ashen face and blank eyes, asked no questions but led her into the sitting room. Carl brought them tea and, in response to his wife's unspoken gesture, shut the door behind them and left the sisters to talk.

Linda sat next to Ali on the sofa and stroked her arm.

"Take your time, love. Just tell me that it's not Lucy."

Ali shook her head.

"OK, then for you to be this upset it must be that wonderful husband of yours. Is it something to do with Jack? Did you spend the night with him on Friday? Is that where you were?"

Ali told Linda about what had happened on Friday night.

"What he said really moved me Lin and then, in the church on Saturday, listening to the words of the ceremony, I decided that it was wrong of me to just walk away from my marriage. All the way back from Devon I kept imagining how pleased he'd be when I told him.

Ali laughed bitterly: "Well, I couldn't have been more wrong. He looked as though the idea repulsed him." Ali's laugh rose hysterically. "He finds me repulsive. Linda. We slept together, you know, on Friday night; twice actually. I wasn't so abhorrent to him then."

"OK look." Linda held Ali's hands. "You're not in any worse position than you were in a few days ago. In fact, you're in a better one because you've had an opportunity to make absolutely sure that you did the right thing in leaving Jack. Now you know. The man's a complete and utter knob."

"Talking about me again, ladies."

Carl came in with a plate of bacon sandwiches. Ali found to her surprise that she was starving and, after eating several, she felt a lot better. The three of them watched TV and, when Ali went upstairs to the spare room, although she lay awake for quite some time, she felt resigned rather than distraught. She had thought that she was over Jack completely but the events of the weekend told her that she still had feelings for him. Once had feelings rather; his coldness towards her today and the cruelty of his words had made her see him in a new light. No longer the loving husband or even the misguided adulterer but someone she didn't know at all and had no wish to know.

Ali's flight back to Spain wasn't until later on the next day and so she and Linda went shopping.

"There's not much a good bargain won't cure," grinned Linda. "Well, either that or something hideously expensive. You didn't manage to swipe Jack's credit card as you left did you? Pity, we'll have to make do with

Carl's."

The sister's giggled and walked arm in arm down the high street. Ali bought two little dresses in readiness for Linda's baby and a jumper for Lucy, which Linda said she'd post for her.

"I was disappointed when Lucy said she'd be away in Dublin this weekend but I'm glad now. I wouldn't have wanted her to see me like this."

Although Ali had brightened up considerably, Linda could tell that her sister had been very hurt by what had happened.

"Did you really feel certain that you wanted Jack back?" she asked.

"I hadn't realised until I saw him how much I still felt for him. I'm not sure how much of it was to do with being at the wedding. Seeing Simon and Cici so much in love and hearing the vows. And there was this lovely old couple in the church holding hands and I thought, well, you know."

"They were probably on their third marriage, Ali," laughed Linda.

"Well, there's not a lot of love left for that man now, I can promise you that, sis."

Linda held up a pair of narrow black jeans with sequins down each leg.

"I couldn't get them past my knees but they'd look great on you. Go on, try them on."

In the changing room Ali looked at her reflection in the mirror. She looked tired but otherwise not too bad and the jeans did suit her long legs. Lee would approve of the sparkles. She thought fondly of her friend in Compesita and of her little house there. It was time to return.

CHAPTER TWENTY-FOUR

Although Lucy had recovered well from her experience with Mason, she was aware of how much she had needed her mother's help to be rid of him and often thought of other women who might not be so lucky to have a loving family to support them. When she saw a poster in the uni bar asking for volunteers at a local women's refuge she took down the number and called the next day.

"I have had some dealings with violent men, well, one violent man and, although I don't have any particular skills, I don't mind helping out with anything really."

The woman from the refuge sounded brisk but friendly, "That's great. Well, there's general work around the house, cooking and cleaning, although the women do a lot themselves. And then they need taking to appointments or the kids need looking after. Sometimes, just having an extra person to sit and listen is really helpful."

Lucy agreed to visit the refuge on Saturday morning. It was housed in a rather depressing brick villa on the outskirts of Bath. Inside, however, the rooms had been painted in bright primary colours and, in the large kitchen, children's paintings had been attached to every surface.

The woman Lucy had spoken to, Maya, introduced her to several women who were sitting drinking tea around a long pine table. Lucy was surprised at how old some of the women were. She had expected to see girls of her own age or a little older but a couple of the women looked to be at least sixty.

Maya showed Lucy the garden where a couple of small children were playing in a sandpit, watched by some more women, huddled by the back door, smoking. There was a shiny new set of swings which Maya said had been donated by a local women's business club.

"Are you OK to stay for a few hours this morning, Lucy?" asked Maya. "We'll need to do the usual checks before you can start here properly but it would be a big help if you could just be here for a little while today. Sue and Pauline need to go down to the law centre. Tom will drive but they'll feel easier if you go as well."

Seeing Lucy's surprised expression Maya added, "Oh, Tom's a sweetie and the women all know him but not all of them are completely relaxed in the presence of men. We couldn't do without him though. He's awfully good at fixing things and the kids love him. Now, if you could just go and help in the kitchen, there's always endless mugs to be washed up, I'll give you a shout in about ten minutes."

As she rinsed the cups at the sink, a short dark-haired woman picked up a tea towel and stood by her, drying each one with exaggerated care. It was one of the older women that Lucy had noticed earlier, although, closer to, she thought that the woman may be closer to fifty than sixty.

"I like to stay in the kitchen so that I can keep an eye on my Harry. That's him there, in the sandpit."

Lucy looked at the small boy pushing a plastic tractor around the sandpit and mentally reduced the woman's age further.

"It's been a blessing, this place. I was knocked about a bit by my husband; he's always done it, to be honest but since I had Harry, it got worse. I started to worry that one day he'd have a go at him but I had nowhere to go; I've no family. When my GP told me about this place, well, I just packed up and left."

Lucy could see Maya beckoning her from the door and, excusing herself, she walked into the hall. Two women were standing next to a tall, very thin young man. His long wavy hair was tied up in a ponytail and he had a curly beard. His eyebrow and his lip were both pierced but, when he smiled, Lucy could see that he had beautiful white teeth and kind, gentle eyes.

"You must be Lucy. Hi, I'm Tom and this is Sue and Pauline. OK, ladies, let's go. Shall we take the Porsche today Pauline or make do with the Fiesta?"

Lucy saw that both Sue and Pauline had bruises on

their faces and she wasn't sure what to say to them as they drove along. Tom, however, did most of the talking and, although neither of the women said much, the atmosphere in the car was relaxed and easy.

"Lucy, if you can just go in with Sue and Pauline, I'll stay with the car. It's not the best of neighbourhoods. They have appointments but there's usually a bit of a wait."

After that first time, Lucy went to help at the refuge twice a week, usually on Wednesday evenings and Saturday mornings. Her favourite times where when she played with the children; either in the garden or, when it rained, at the kitchen table helping the children paint messy pictures or play dog eared old board games. The children could be quite difficult; some were sullen and withdrawn whilst others were attention seeking and hyper-active. Almost all of them were manipulative, even the quieter ones and Maya explained to Lucy that this was often the case with children who came from abusive homes; they'd learned the need to protect themselves.

Another reason why she liked being with the children was that Tom often helped her, joining in their games, giving them piggy back rides and making them squeal with laughter. All of the children loved Tom and vied for his attention. Lucy often found herself doing something similar. He was so charismatic and full of life and yet he also had a calmness about him; a stillness at his centre.

Tom had a long beaked nose that prevented him from being handsome but somehow it suited his face and Lucy could watch him for hours, seeing how patient and kind he was with everyone. She was fascinated by his long wavy hair. Usually it was tied back but one day a couple of the little girls persuaded him to let them play with it and he sat at the kitchen table like a romantic poet with his hair cascading over his shoulders.

There was never much time to talk at the refuge but Lucy always volunteered to go with Tom when he drove the women to various appointments and, as they sat and waited, she found out a little about his life. He told her that he was working on a building site and that he wanted to learn skills so that he could go and work for a charity abroad.

"They tease me at the site about my hair and piercings. I don't mind really; I'm learning a lot and that's why I'm there. And it keeps me fit, look."

Lucy watched as Tom pushed up the sleeve of his T-shirt and flexed his biceps.

"I don't know why I just did that. You must think I'm a right arse pretending to be a macho man."

Tom smiled ruefully and Lucy wondered what it would feel like to be kissed by a man with a beard. She realised that Tom was speaking again, "Sorry, what? Oh yes, the women should be out soon."

One Saturday as she was leaving the refuge after her morning shift, Tom called to her from his battered old car. "Are you doing anything now, Lucy? It' such a beautiful day I was wondering if you'd like to go for a walk or something. Maybe get some lunch? If you're not busy that is."

Lucy silently thanked God that she'd made the effort to get up early that morning and wash her hair although she wished that she'd bothered to iron her new jeans instead of pulling on her oldest ones. She jumped into the passenger seat and tried, unsuccessfully, to stop herself from grinning too broadly. Tom turned to her, "Tell you what, how about a picnic? If you don't mind waiting a bit, I'll stop at my place and grab a few things to eat."

Tom had told her that he lived with his parents but had seemed reluctant to elaborate and Lucy hadn't wanted to pry. He had said that his father worked away a lot and the tone of his voice made Lucy wonder if in fact Tom's Dad was actually in prison or something. There obviously wasn't a lot of money. Tom's car was barely roadworthy and he always wore the same narrow black jeans and work boots. His mobile phone was cheap and basic; he'd told

155

Lucy that, whenever possible, he preferred to wait until he could talk to a person face to face. Although Lucy had understood what he meant, she couldn't imagine being without her smart phone, at least not for more than five minutes.

When they pulled up outside a smart house in a Georgian terrace, Lucy was astonished. In her mind she'd pictured a run-down semi with a jacked up car in the garden and Tom's mother wearily smoking a fag at the front door. Tom told her that he'd just be a few minutes and ran, long leggedly, down some steps that Lucy assumed led to a basement flat. Even a flat in this street would cost a fortune and Lucy wondered if Tom's mother was perhaps a housekeeper, permitted to share the basement with her son and, when released from his frequent bouts of incarceration, her husband. If Tom's mother was a housekeeper then hopefully the picnic would be good. She had envisaged Dairylea sandwiches and Kit Kats and, rather reluctantly, let that image go.

They had a magical day. Tom drove them to a park by the river which she hadn't been to before and his picnic of cheddar cheese, oatcakes and apples was perfect. He'd even brought a rather good Sancerre and Lucy hoped Tom wouldn't get into trouble when his mother's employers noticed the raid on their wine cellar.

After they'd eaten they lay side by side on the grass and Tom asked her questions about her childhood. When she told him about her parent's separation and seemingly inevitable divorce, tears came into her eyes and Tom, tentatively at first but then with increasing firmness, leant over and kissed her. His beard felt soft against her chin, not prickly as she'd imagined. She felt her whole body responding and her mind was full of joy. So, this is what it felt like to kiss Tom.

He smiled into her eyes: "You know, the first time I saw you standing at the kitchen sink at the refuge, I thought that you were one of the women in need of shelter.

I hate all violence but somehow the idea of some man hurting you made me feel crazy."

Lucy told Tom about her awful time with Mason. She wanted to tell him everything about herself. Holding hands, they wandered here and there down the narrow streets. The world suddenly seemed full of possibility and happiness to Lucy. She wanted to smile at everyone they passed. Walking beside this tall, lanky man, stopping every now and then to exchange kisses, pointing out things to one another; a china dog in the window of an antique shop that Lucy said looked just like Tom, two old ladies convulsed with laughter outside a café, everything felt absolutely right. She knew that, when she was alone, she would relive these hours in her mind again and again and remember them as something completely perfect.

When it grew dark it seemed natural for Tom to say, "Shall we go back to my place tonight?" and for Lucy to agree.

She wondered, briefly, whether his mother would be at the flat but thought that she may be upstairs, cooking diner for her employers. She added Tom's father to the scene, serving the main course from large silver platters before shaking her head and giggling; she was letting her imagination run away with her.

"What are you laughing at, Lucy?" Tom asked, smiling down at her.

"Oh nothing. I just feel happy, that's all."

"Me too. Utterly, crazily happy and that's all your fault."

The basement steps led straight into a bedroom. Tom lit a lamp and Lucy noticed that the large square room was plainly furnished. There was a double bed with an Indian cotton throw, a desk, a couple of bookcases and, beside the window, an armchair. The walls were bare except for an oil painting of a seascape. Before Lucy could take a closer look, Tom reached for her hand and pulled her onto the bed. He lay on his side beside her, his long fingers stroking the contours of her face. He told her that she was beautiful and then, very slowly and gently, began to make love to her.

Lucy's only experience of sex had been with Mason. He had been her first lover and, although Mason denied it, she suspected that she'd been his too. Whereas Mason had been hasty and eager, Tom was sensual and caring. He explored every part of her body, returning to kiss her mouth and gaze deeply into her eyes. For the first time she felt the power of her woman's body and she responded to his touch with an unselfconsciousness which surprised her. After a while his love-making became fiercer and more animalistic and Lucy found that this was what she wanted too and she clung to him, following his rhythm.

When she woke up in the morning, Tom wasn't there and Lucy could hear a shower going in an adjacent bathroom. She stretched luxuriously and thought of last night. She could hardly wait for Tom to return and she realised, with a sudden flood of happiness, that there would be many nights and mornings to share with this man.

Later that morning, after they'd made love again and Tom had brought them tea and toast to eat in bed, Tom said, "Well I suppose we'd better go upstairs and say hello to my parents."

Lucy's heart raced: "Oh, they're both here are they? Your Dad, too?"

Tom grinned: "Don't look so worried. They're not too bad really. And they'll adore you. I adore you."

It was another hour before Lucy finally made it into the bathroom to shower and dress before meeting Tom's parents. The bathroom was modern and stylish, with a powerful walk in shower and plush fluffy towels. Whoever owned this place was clearly wealthy. Lucy looked at her reflection in the bathroom mirror. She had her father's thick blonde hair which she wore in a short tousled cut. She also had Jack's straight nose but her eyes were green, like her mother's.

A door on the far side of Tom's bedroom led into a

corridor which housed a small galley kitchen and, at the end, as set of stars leading to the ground floor. Holding Tom's hand, Lucy climbed upwards and emerged into the hallway of the main house. Tom led her through a set of double doors into a wonderfully bright and spacious room which ran the length of the house. To her left was a modern kitchen with shiny white cupboards and doors opening onto a small courtyard garden. The other part of the room faced the road and, sitting in the beautiful tall Georgian window, was a woman who could only have been Tom's mother. She was tall and slim with Tom's hooked nose and gentle eyes. Her short hair was tucked behind her ears, revealing elegant gold earrings and she wore an expensive looking crisp white shirt tucked into narrow black jeans.

"Good morning, darling. Who's this?"

She came over to give Tom a kiss.

"Mum, Dad, this is my friend Lucy. Lucy, my parents, Ann and Hugh."

Lucy stepped forwards and shook Ann's hand before turning to look at the man rising from an armchair by the fireplace. As he walked towards her, Lucy could see that he was shorter and burlier than Tom but his hair, although short and receding, was the same colour as his son's. He smiled at her with amused grey eyes.

"Hello, Lucy. It's very nice to meet you. Would you like some coffee or a glass of wine maybe? It's very nearly midday."

Hugh had an intensity about him that Lucy recognised in Tom, although Tom had a calm presence which this man lacked. There was an impatience in the way he moved and spoke.

Accepting coffee, Lucy complimented Ann and Hugh on the room and turned to raise her eyebrows at Tom: "You didn't tell me, Tom, that you lived in such a lovely house." It was wonderful, light and airy with contemporary furniture and paintings and photographs everywhere. Over the fireplace was an oil painting of a rainy street and, seeing Lucy looking at it, Ann said, "Do you like it? It's one of my favourites."

"Is it by the same artist as the sea scape in Tom's room?" Lucy asked, blushing faintly at the thought of the two of them lying in each other's arms whilst this elegant pair breakfasted above.

"How clever of you to notice, Lucy. Yes, my brother did them both. We have several more of his. Would you like a tour? Come on, bring your coffee."

On the first floor there was another, more formal sitting room and two studies; one for each parent Lucy assumed. There were two more floors containing bedrooms and bathrooms, all beautifully decorated and furnished.

"This is my perfect house," said Lucy.

"That's so kind of you to say so. It was in a bit of a state when Hugh and I bought it but I could see the potential. There's a lot of stairs though. Hugh has to keep a pair of reading glasses on each floor."

"How long have you lived here?"

"We moved in just before Tom was born. I'm sure that's the reason he's working at a building site now; all those early memories of hammering and banging."

Ann smiled but Lucy could see the tension in her face.

"And as we already had Mathew and Kat, we needed more space. The garden's not large but it made it easier to keep an eye on them when they were small. Tom was an absolute horror."

Lucy thought about how little she knew of Tom's life. She'd completely misread his home situation, although he'd definitely been intentionally ambiguous. She hadn't even known that he had a brother and sister. She was tempted to ask more questions of his mother but the person she really needed to talk to was Tom himself.

Although Ann asked Tom and Lucy to stay for lunch, Lucy had an essay to finish and so they left to drive back to her shared house on the other side of Bath. After spending such an intense twenty-four hours with Tom, so much had happened in that short time that Lucy felt her spirits dropping at the thought of being without him. When he suggested that they stop on the way for a late breakfast, she readily agreed. It would delay their parting and give her an opportunity to get Tom to tell her more about himself.

They found a café in a quiet side street and ordered scrambled eggs and coffee.

"I liked your parents, Tom, but I have to say they were not at all what I was expecting; nor was your house."

Tom smiled ruefully and reached over to stroke her wrist with his thumb. "I've got used to not really telling people where I live. I don't want the lads on the site to think I'm showing off or something. I just want to be treated like one of them. I'm sorry, Lucy, I didn't mean to mislead you. Ask me anything you like. What do you want to know?"

"Everything, Tom. I want to know everything about you."

CHAPTER TWENTY-FIVE

On the morning after Ali arrived back in Compesita she went round to see Lee. Ali was surprised and disappointed to find her friend packing. Noticing her fallen expression, Lee said regretfully, "I know, Ali, but we've already stayed a month longer than we'd planned. Our son is struggling a bit with the business and he really needs our support. Des has already left."

Lee tried unsuccessfully to zip up a suitcase and sighed, "I can't believe how many shoes I seem to have bought. I don't think we're the same size are we, Ali? Otherwise you could have had some."

Ali looked doubtfully at Lee's tiny feet. Seeing the shoe boxes scattered around reminded Ali of the disaster at the wedding and she told Lee the story of the landlady's shoes.

"It sounds as though you had a good time." Lee looked anxiously at her friend: "Did anything else happen? Did you bump into your ex?"

"Well actually I did but it was a complete and utter disaster. I made such of a fool of myself, Lee."

"OK, this sounds to me like a bottle story; possibly two bottles."

Ali and Lee sat in the autumn sunshine on Lee's terrace and Ali told her what had happened with Jack. When she had finished Lee went to fetch another bottle of wine and said, "You know, Ali, I think that what your sister said was right. Part of you was obviously still wondering if there was a chance of saving your marriage and, if you felt like that and Jack clearly thought so too, then I'd have done what you did. I think most women would."

Lee continued: "What I can't understand is why he changed his mind so quickly. That seems really odd to me?"

Ali took a sip of wine: "I've thought about that a lot, as you can imagine. The only sense I can make of it is that he always wants what he hasn't got; once he does get it, he no longer wants it. I think also that part of him was quite enjoying being the heartbroken husband; I think he liked the drama of it all. Once the possibility of us going back to normal became a reality, it was no longer exciting for him.

"He always was a man who looked for the next adventure, the next fun. Last Christmas, when we were eating the turkey, he said 'I know, let's have goose next year.' He couldn't just enjoy the moment. And his mother spoilt him, of course."

The women looked at each other and laughed: "It's always some woman's fault isn't it?" said Lee.

Although it was now over four months since the start of Ali's sabbatical, she still hadn't decided what she wanted to do with her life. After the recent events with Jack, she was sure that she never wanted to live in their cottage again and she would arrange for it to be put on the market as soon as possible. They'd paid off the mortgage a few years ago and there should be enough for her to be able to buy another property with her half of the money.

As for her job, the safest option would be to return to Cassell Brookes and Little and resume her career. However, Ali was tempted by the offer she'd had from her old client John Drake. She'd still be using her skills but in a different environment. She could live where she liked; move to be nearer to Linda maybe or even stay part of the year in Compesita. Another alternative would be to move to a larger legal firm, in London possibly. The work would be challenging and the hours long but the pay would be good and it would be a fresh start for her. Sometimes Ali felt that she'd like to do something completely different. She'd always enjoyed cooking and so maybe she could work in a restaurant. Money would be a factor though; she'd managed really well on a tight budget in recent months but doing it long term may not be so easy.

Her thoughts often kept her awake at night and she made endless lists with the advantages and disadvantages of each option. To take her mind off the future, Ali decided to ask the people she was learning Spanish with to come round one evening for tapas. Although Ali still had private lessons with her neighbour Mary, she'd also joined a group session which met once a week in a local bar. They were quite a diverse collection of people but Ali enjoyed the meetings and they usually stayed and had a drink afterwards.

On the day of the party, Ali drove to the next town to stock up on wine and ingredients for the tapas. She ran into Paul's sister, Jan, who was staying at her villa for a few days and invited her for lunch the next day. Back at her house, Ali enjoyed preparing the tapas. She laid out platters of Manchego cheese and Serrano Ham to have with crusty bread and garlic mayonnaise. Large local tomatoes she simply sliced and drizzled with olive oil. She also made a pork and pepper stew and some prawns wrapped in chorizo.

As Casa Lucia was so tiny, she decided to let her guests wander over the whole house and, if it was warm enough, into the garden. Just before everyone was due to arrive, Ali lit all of the lamps and laid out bowels of almonds and olives. The Spanish group all arrived promptly. There were ten of them in all, including Ali and Mary. There were only two men; the husband of one of the women who hardly uttered a word but who always made copious notes and Martin, the only single man.

Ali was always amused to see the attention that Martin received from the women in the group. He was a short, portly man in his early sixties who wrote very bad poetry which he would read aloud given the slightest encouragement and often when he wasn't. Martin usually managed to sit next to Ali when they had their group sessions in the village bar and, whenever he said something correctly, he would turn to see if Ali had noticed.

Finding that Martin seemed inclined to hover in the kitchen where she was finishing off the tapas, Ali gave him the platters of ham and cheese to hand out and he waddled off proudly, like a schoolboy who'd been asked to help his teacher.

It was a slightly chilly evening and so most of the guests gathered in the upstairs area, near the kitchen. It was rather crowded but everyone seemed to be enjoying themselves and Ali walked around topping up glasses and listening to snippets of conversation. One person in the Spanish group invariably sought to dominate every session and she behaved no differently at the party. Catherine was tall and stoutly built with lots of black hair which was always pinned up with two tortoiseshell combs. At some time in her past she'd worked for a film director and she in variably introduced some allusion to the film industry into every conversation.

Catherine's knowledge of Spanish, although reasonable, wasn't as good as she thought it was; a fact that didn't prevent her from correcting Mary's pronunciation. If Catherine didn't know a Spanish word or phrase, she'd often tell the class what it would be in French, much to Ali's annoyance.

Catherine's strident voice rose above the murmur of conversation. "Make way, make way. Here I am with fresh supplies."

Ali had noticed that the plates of tapas had disappeared alarmingly quickly but, as the party was drawing to a close and people were starting to say goodbye, she hadn't been too worried. Now she stared in astonishment as Catherine emerged from the kitchen holding aloft two plates piled high with prawns and smoked salmon; the lunch Ali had bought for Jan tomorrow.

"I found this in the fridge, Ali. You'd forgotten to bring it out and I could see that everyone was still hungry." Catherine leered at Martin. "Especially the menfolk. It's so important to keep the food flowing. You know, when I was in the…"

Catherine pursed her lips and, glancing at Ali, tossed her head and said gaily, "Anyway, dig in people.

165

Catherine's saved the day."

Ali seethed; how typical of the bloody woman to assume control at the expense of someone else. Her anger only increased when she saw that, as everyone had begun to leave, the plates of expensive seafood where largely ignored. Catherine came over to say goodbye: "It seems to be winding down. Just as well; you look a little tired, my dear. Now, don't forget to put those platters back in the fridge, will you? You don't want them to go to waste."

The next morning was unusually cold and wet and Ali, having stayed up late the night before to clear up after the party, couldn't face driving to the supermarket again. She bought some fresh bread and local tomatoes and cheese at the village shop and rushed home in the rain to wait for Jan. She hadn't seen her since her first visit to Compesita earlier in the year, although she'd become very fond of Jan's brother Paul.

Ali had tried to speak to Paul before she'd left Compesita to go to Simon's wedding. He'd clearly thought that she'd been having a relationship with Robert and she'd wanted to put him right. However, when she'd called at Jan's house, where Paul had been staying, there was no one in. She'd considered leaving a note but hadn't been able to think what to write. She could hardly have said, *Sorry I missed you. See you soon. Ali.*
PS I didn't sleep with Robert.
PPS In case you thought that I did.
PPPS You probably didn't, so just ignore this.

The rain cleared up around noon and the sun shone. Ali brought the lunch outside and she and Jan sat at the iron table in the garden.

"It's lovely to sit and relax for a while," said Jan, leaning back to hold her face into the sun. "I've done nothing but clean since I got here. Juanita normally has the place ready for me but I haven't seen her since I arrived. I hope Paul didn't do anything to offend her. Did he

166

mention anything to you?"

Ali wanted to laugh, thinking of the performance she and Paul put on to convince Juanita that she was Paul's fiancée, but she shook her head.

"Oh well, I'll sort it out next time I'm here. Paul will have to iron his own shirts when he comes back out; it won't kill him."

"I thought I hadn't seen him around. Is he coming over soon?"

Ali tried to sound casual but she felt quite excited at the thought of seeing Paul again.

"In a few weeks. He's had some issues to sort out back home but we're all optimistic that everything will be cleared up soon."

Ali raised her eyebrows: "Oh, nothing serious I hope?"

"Well, we'll see. Anyway, tell me about last night. How did it go?"

When Jan left, Ali asked her to give her love to Paul and to tell him that she was looking forward to seeing him again. Earlier she'd told Jan about the stay at La Cumbre with Robert, making it sound as though she was merely telling an amusing story but really hoping that Jan would relay it to her brother. Now that Jack was truly out of her life for good, Ali thought that she'd like to get to know Paul a little, or a lot, better.

CHAPTER TWENTY-SIX

"You'll have to speak to her. She's been doing it again. In the kitchen. I can smell it."

Carl snuggled closer to Linda and put his hand gently on her swollen stomach.

"You used to smoke in the kitchen, Lin. What am I supposed to do? Tell her to go outside?"

"Yes, tell her exactly that. It's not fair, Carl. It's bad enough having her here without her stinking the place out."

"OK, I'll have a word with her. I thought I might take her to the cinema tomorrow night. Do you want to come?"

"God no, she'll only want to see something awful about pensioners falling in love or something. Go for a meal afterwards, I'll enjoy some time on my own."

It was only the third day of Jean's, Carl's Mum's, two-week visit and Linda already felt like murdering her. The idea had been that Jean would help to spring-clean the house before the baby arrived but, as far as Linda could tell, all she'd done so far was to watch daytime TV and drink tea. On her first night Carl had been held up at the school where he worked and so Linda had collected her from the station and then gone into the kitchen to prepare their evening meal. Jean had said she felt tired from her journey and was going for a lie down.

Linda, by now quite heavily pregnant and exhausted after a long day at work, felt aggrieved and chopped vegetables furiously. The bloody woman wasn't much older than she was and yet she was acting like an eighty-year-old. She was even more annoyed when Jean, hearing Carl's key in the lock, ran down into the kitchen and picked up a tea towel, just in time for Carl's entrance.

"Carl, my boy. Come here, son. You're looking a bit peaky. Are you eating properly? How do I look? I've had my hair done. Do you like it? Ouch."

Linda had snatched the tea towel from Jean's fingers,

earning her a puzzled look from Carl.

"I'm fine, Mum and, yes, your hair looks great. So, how's my darling?"

Both Linda and Jean answered together and Carl gave a nervous laugh.

After that, things didn't get any better. Jean constantly made references to Linda's weight, telling her that she'd struggle to lose it once the baby was born.

"I hardly put on an ounce with our Carl. People couldn't believe I was pregnant. And afterwards I was straight back into my normal clothes. I'm often complimented on my figure, aren't I, Carl?"

Jean smoothed down her skirt and looked coyly at her son. Linda seethed; not so much about the reference to her weight but she knew that Carl was uncomfortable when his mother behaved in this way. He'd told her that, when he was a teenager, his mother used to ask him if he thought she looked pretty or if a certain outfit suited her, and it had embarrassed him.

On Friday morning Linda left for work gladly, although she was dreading the weekend ahead with Jean. At half past eleven the phone on Linda's desk rang: "Mrs Mathews? It's Mr Patel here, from the corner shop. I'm afraid that your mother-in-law has been caught trying to steal some items. I saw her quite clearly on my security monitor. I was going to call the police but she became very agitated. She asked me to call you."

"Oh no, Mr Patel, I am so sorry. Please don't call the police. I'll come straight over. What? Oh, OK, tell her that I won't speak to my husband just yet."

Luckily, Carl and Linda believed in buying as much as they could in their local shops and were regular customers of Mr Patel's general store. Given that, and Mrs Patel's plea that her husband be lenient, he agreed not to call the police and allowed a distraught Jean to leave with Linda. Back at home, Linda made them both a cup of tea and sat Jean down at the kitchen table.

"Why on earth did you do it, Jean? You're not short of

money are you?"

Jean stared at her daughter-in-law with red rimmed eyes and put her hand to her mouth, "I don't know what came over me, Linda. One minute I was looking at the shelves and the next I was outside the shop with that Indian man grabbing my arm."

Jean clutched Linda's hand, "Please, please don't say a word to Carl. He doesn't have to know. I couldn't bear it."

She started sobbing again. Linda's head began to throb.

"You know what he's like, Linda. I just couldn't stand it if he felt ashamed of me."

Linda knew Carl to be the most forgiving of men but he did have a very strict moral code. There were things in her past which Linda hadn't been able to bring herself to tell him. And she didn't want him to worry; he was already anxious enough about her and the baby.

"No, OK, perhaps he doesn't need to know. As long as you promise me that you'll never do anything like this again."

Jean looked up at her with grateful eyes, "Never, I swear on Carl's life. Thank you, oh thank you, Linda."

Linda made them another cup of tea and they went through into the sitting room.

"When Carl's father left, Carl was all I had. We were so close. He was my little man. I've just been a bit lonely, you see, after Carl came to London and then married you. And now the baby's coming and he'll have a new family of his own. He doesn't need me now."

Linda took a deep breath. She knew that Jean had struggled to bring Carl up on her own after her husband walked out. Although she hadn't been the best of mothers, Carl loved her and it can't have been easy for him when Linda was openly hostile towards her.

"Look, we do need you, Jean, of course we do. When the baby's born, I'll expect you to help out a lot. You're the one with experience. I haven't a clue. I'll probably give it the wrong food or drop it or something. And my Mum isn't here to help me so I'd really appreciate it if you could."

As she said this Linda realised that it was true. She dearly missed having her mother around to advise her during her pregnancy and had wished many times that she was still alive to see her granddaughter born. Jean was very different to her own mother but, she'd brought up Carl, and she hadn't done so badly there.

"Really? Do you mean that? Oh, Linda, I'd be delighted. I'd be so proud to be involved."

When Carl arrived home from school that evening he was astonished to find his wife and mother sitting together on the sofa looking at an old photograph album of Jean's.

"I can't believe you let him out in that outfit, Jean. What were you thinking?"

"I know, he looks just like a girl."

Both women laughed gleefully, their heads touching as they turned the pages.

"Oh no! Look at that hat. Will you knit one like that for the baby, Jean? Please."

"Knit one? I've still got the original one at home – Ha ha ha."

CHAPTER TWENTY-SEVEN

A week after her lunch with Jan, Ali was delighted to see Paul standing outside Casa Lucia one morning; she hadn't expected him to return so soon. He had a small brown dog with him on a lead.

"Freddie and I wondered if you'd like to go for a walk with us?"

Ali smiled at them both: "Freddie? Is that Mary's dog?"

"Yes, I found him in her garden next door looking a bit fed up. I think Mary insists on talking to him in Spanish and he can't understand a word she says."

Ali laughed: "Yes, she does that with me too. I had the most confusing conversation with her the other day. She was either telling me that her uncle had died or that she wanted a dry sherry. I really wasn't sure which. I gave her a sherry anyway; I thought it covered both options."

The day was cool but bright and they wandered slowly through the village, Freddie stopping to examine every tree. Eventually, he led them to the corner bar and flopped under a table, panting heavily.

"Crafty old Mary," said Ali. "I often wondered why her walks with Freddie took so long."

They both ordered coffee and Ali watched as Paul sat down and leant back in his chair. He looked a little thinner than the last time she'd seen him.

"Jan mentioned that you were having some problem or other at home. Has it been sorted out now?"

"Not completely but I've done all I can and so I thought I may as well come out here."

"Do you want to talk about it?"

Paul smiled at her. "Yes, I'd like to but not right now, if that's OK. I've already told Freddie and we don't want to bore him to death, do we, Fred? Come on, let's head back. So, what have you been up to, Ali? Spent any more nights in posh hotels?"

When Ali stopped to look at him, Paul grinned: "Jan

told me all about the trip with Robert and his car and everything. Actually, you'll laugh when you hear this but I thought that you and he were an item, before I knew the full story that is. I should have known better, as if you'd ever date a bloke who wears pink trousers."

"He's a very attractive man, at least, he thinks so."

Paul turned to face Ali. He stood very close to her and looked in her eyes, "There's only one attractive man around here."

"Oh, I agree," murmured Ali. "You're gorgeous, aren't you, Fred?"

Paul asked Ali if she'd come over to Jan's villa that evening, promising to cook her a meal. As she got ready Ali wondered if anything would happen between them tonight; she knew that Paul liked her. She decided to call Emma and ask her advice. After they had discussed what she should wear, Emma said, "You may have to take the initiative, Ali. Dating has changed since you were last single. Women ask men out now."

"I did try to kiss him once before, but he turned me down. I was very drunk, it has to be said."

"Mmmm, a man with ethics. This may be harder than I thought. You'll have to make it very clear that you're up for it."

"I don't much like the sound of that. Whatever happened to romance and roses?"

Emma sighed: "Oh dear, you are out of the loop, aren't you? Look, do you want to get him into bed or not? Here's what I suggest…"

Jan's villa looked even lovelier than the last time Ali had seen it, with tall lamps casting a golden glow over the garden. Paul, looking extremely attractive in jeans and a pale blue linen shirt, had laid the table in the large kitchen. He'd turned off the main lights and put candles everywhere.

"We won't be able to see what we're eating but, I can

assure you, that's a good thing."

"What are we having? It smells delicious," said Ali, handing Paul a bottle of Rioja she'd brought.

She, too, was looking good in a cream silk blouse and a short black skirt. Emma had suggested it, saying: "You've got fantastic legs, Ali, you may as well show them off."

Seeing Paul look at her appreciatively, Ali was glad she had taken her friend's advice. Emma had also told her to get the first kiss out of the way as soon as possible and so, after accepting a glass of Cava, Ali walked over to Paul and kissed him on the mouth. The kiss only lasted for a couple of seconds but, as they pulled apart and looked at one another, they both knew that their friendship was going to turn into something that night.

Paul had cooked chicken in a tarragon cream sauce and they lingered over their meal, enjoying each other's company. Later on they carried their wine glasses into the large lounge and sat together on one of the low sofas. Paul picked up Ali's glass and put it on the floor before pulling her towards him and kissing her. This kiss lasted longer than a few seconds. Paul put one hand on her back and pressed her firmly against his chest. With his other hand he stroked her hair.

Ali had forgotten how wonderful kissing was. She and Jack kissed, of course, but it had been ages, years even, since she'd spent quite so long just enjoying the sensation of someone's lips against hers. She ran her hands down his arms and across his back. Paul was smaller in build than Jack, his back narrower but his body felt taut and muscular.

Paul's hand fell from her hair and he began to squeeze her breast, circling his thumb over her nipple. Ali hungrily reached for his mouth again, flickering her tongue against his. Suddenly Paul pulled away.

"Ali, before we go any further, there's something I must say."

Oh God no, thought Ali, *surely he's not going to go all moralistic on me again. Can't he see that I want this?*

174

At that moment her phone rang and, glancing into her handbag, she saw it was her sister Linda. She sat up. "Sorry, but I have to take this. It's my sister Linda. She's having a baby quite soon. I'll just make sure everything's OK."

Ali got up and walked over to the window. Having established that Linda was fine and had just wanted to chat, Ali ended the call as quickly as she could. Turning from the window, she walked slowly and, she hoped, seductively towards Paul, unbuttoning her blouse as she went. As she reached the sofa, she unzipped her skirt and stepped out of it, standing before him in nothing but her black lace underwear. She crouched down and whispered in his ear, "Now then, what did you want to say or can it wait?"

CHAPTER TWENTY-EIGHT

In the month since Simon's wedding, Emma had kept her promise to herself and had tried not to think of him and Cici together on honeymoon or living cosily in Simon's flat. She'd booked a week's walking holiday in Derbyshire and had made sure that her weekends and evenings were filled with activity. A man in the audit department of the bank had asked her out to dinner but she hadn't been able to bring herself to accept; not quite yet.

When Simon called her at work one Friday afternoon and asked if he could come over that evening, she hesitated at first. In the old, pre-Cici days, they'd often spent whole weekends together, visiting markets and galleries and cooking meals in Emma's kitchen. Now he was married, she'd accepted that those days were over and she was a little surprised at his request. However, she had missed him and, just because he was married, it didn't mean that they couldn't still be friends. She asked him to come round at any time after eight.

It was just like old times. They put on cheesy '80s pop music and danced around the kitchen. Simon cooked the pasta whilst Emma made the sauce. They opened a bottle of their favourite red wine and sat side by side at the table, gossiping about mutual friends. Simon drank quite a lot of wine. Before, he'd have stayed the night in Emma's spare room but she assumed he'd be going home to Cici tonight.

He'd been strangely reticent about their honeymoon. Normally, when Simon returned from holiday, he'd be full of amusing stories.

"Where's Cici this evening?"

Simon waved his hand, "Oh, she's gone to her parents for the weekend. I suggested she go." He turned to look at Emma: "Actually, Em, I felt that I need a break. She's a lovely girl but lovely gets on your nerves after a while; sometimes you want a bit more edge, you know?"

Emma said nothing and Simon was encouraged to

continue: "I think I may have made a mistake, in marrying Cici I mean. I'm not sure that I'm the kind of man who should be married. I don't think it suits me. Do you think it suits me, Em?"

Emma stood up and waited for a moment before replying. Simon continued to drink his wine, whilst looking up at Emma expectantly.

"Well you did marry her, Simon, and now you've got to try and make it work. It's only been a few weeks. You can't expect to adapt to marriage after living on your own for so long without having a few problems."

Simon's face fell. He'd been so sure that Emma would tell him that he was right and that he should never have got married. Emma continued: "She's a nice girl and she's madly in love with you. Give her a chance, Simon. Try not to be so, well, so selfish."

Simon put his glass down and said huffily, "If that's how you feel then I'd better leave. I had expected more support from my oldest friend."

Emma managed to persuade him to stay the night. She said that she loved him and that they could talk it through again in the morning.

As she got undressed for bed, Emma wondered why she had encouraged Simon to stay with Cici. If he'd left, she and Simon could have gone back to their old life. With a sudden clarity Emma saw that she wanted more than that for herself and she was looking forward to getting it.

Linda was having a coffee with an old work colleague who'd left a year ago to retrain as a counsellor and who now worked in a university.

"I love the work, Linda, and the students are great. It's not always easy though. There's a girl at the moment who's made a complaint about one of her lecturers."

She leant forward: "I shouldn't really say this but I think she may have made it all up. She's very attention seeking, very manipulative. Her parents have recently been divorced, it's a classic case. However, my job is to speak for her. Whatever the facts are, she needs my help and support."

"I do feel sorry for the chap though, if it does turn out to be untrue that is. You know what people are like. I don't suppose he'll find it easy to progress further in his department. It's not fair but there it is. The head of the history department is keen on women's rights. She wants to re-name it the 'Herstory Department'; can you believe it?"

They ordered another coffee and chatted about other things but Linda couldn't shake off a slight feeling of unease and, as she was saying goodbye, she asked her friend, "This bloke, the one who's in all this trouble, what's his name?"

That evening Linda asked Carl what she should do.

"I'm sure it's not him, Carl. I don't know what Paul's second name is or which university he works at. There must be hundreds of history lecturers."

"You have to find out, Lin. If it is him, then he is clearly a sexual predator and Ali needs to know."

Linda had listened to Ali on the telephone only yesterday telling her about the night she'd spent with Paul, her voice sounding happier than she had in ages and she dreaded the thought of bringing her bad news. However, Ali was really quite inexperienced when it came to men. This Paul sounded nice enough but, if he had slept with one of his students, a girl much younger than him, then she'd have to tell Ali.

Ali needed no encouragement to talk about Paul with her sister. She told her proudly which university he lectured at and added, "His surname is Reading, why?"

Linda's heart had sunk at Ali's replies; she had no option now but to tell her sister what she had found out.

"That's all I know, Ali. He's been suspended whilst the university look into it. Obviously, if what this girl says is true and he did sleep with her then he'll lose his job. It may not be true, of course, but why would she lie?"

Ali's voice was very flat on the other end of the line, "I don't know."

"And he hasn't said anything to you about it?"

"No, nothing at all."

After Linda had rung off, Ali sat on her bed for a long time. It couldn't be true, could it? The Paul that she had spent the night with and who'd been such a tender and caring lover. Had he been involved with one of his students? A girl who must be half his age; Lucy's age in fact. But, if it wasn't true, then why didn't he tell her about it? How could he let their relationship develop and not share this with her?

She thought back to the night they'd slept together. He had said then that he had something to tell her; perhaps this was it? Ali considered calling him but she needed to look at his face when she confronted him. He was supposed to be calling round the next morning; she'd talk to him then.

"So I wanted to call you and let you know straight away. She's admitted that she made the whole thing up and she'd signed a statement to that effect. It seems as though she's done something similar before with an art teacher at her old school. She's left the university now. Her parents have taken her away somewhere."

"And that's it really, Paul. Your nightmare is over. Anyway, take a break and come in and see me when you're back in the UK. We can discuss details then."

Paul put the phone down and sat back in his chair. The reality of the Dean's words suddenly hit him and he was flooded with euphoria and relief. To have her admit that she'd made the whole thing up was the best possible outcome. Even if the university review had exonerated him people would always have wondered if there was something in her story. He put his hands over his mouth and gave a whoop of glee. The happiness that he'd felt being with Ali a few nights ago had, until today, been tinged with darkness. Now, he could let their love grow without limits. He picked up his car keys and headed for the door. Seeing his reflection in the hall mirror he stopped in amazement; he looked ten years younger.

Ali watched from the upstairs window as Paul got out of his car. He was smiling broadly and holding a bunch of flowers. Her heart lurched; it was so unfair. She'd felt so happy the past few days until she'd received Linda's call. Why did every man she met turn out to be such a rat? Angry tears sprang into her eyes. She hardly slept last night and, when she did, she'd dreamt that Paul had seduced Lucy and that Jack had shot him dead.

"Hello. Ali? Are you there? It's me Paul. Shall I come up?"

Ali had prepared an opening question but, when he bounded up the stairs and looked at her so lovingly, she burst into tears and simply said, "When were you going to tell me about the student?"

Paul stood still.

"Oh God, you know? How?"

"It doesn't matter. Is it true?"

"No! Of course it's not true. And she'd admitted it. The Dean's just phoned me. She's admitted making the whole thing up."

Paul put his hands over his face and his voice broke, "I've been living with this for months. I can't believe it's over. Please just come here and give me a hug. I can't bear to see you looking at me like that."

Ali walked over and put her arms around him. Her eyes were shiny with tears.

"But why didn't you tell me? You can trust me surely?"

"I wanted to so many times. I tried to tell you the other night before your phone rang; do you remember? And then you took all your clothes off and I couldn't think straight. That night with you was so wonderful. I couldn't help worrying that, if I told you, you wouldn't believe me; not really. That you'd always wonder if there was some truth in it. And I'd just found you, Ali. I couldn't bear to lose you so soon. I was hoping that it would be at least six months until you realised what an idiot I really am."

Paul still had his arms around Ali and he very gently kissed her teary eyes before moving his mouth more firmly onto her lips. In between kisses he murmured softly, "Are you still wearing that extremely tiny underwear?"

Ali giggled, "Actually, I'm wearing my oldest, biggest pants and I've got a ladder in the top of my tights; want to see?"

"Oooh tights, yes please, you naughty thing."

Later that afternoon they collected Freddie and took him for another walk, this time up beyond the village where it was quiet and peaceful. They stopped to rest at the top of a hill and Ali sat with her back against Paul's legs, enjoying the view and the warmth of his body against hers.

"Promise me there'll be no more secrets between us, Paul. I've had enough secrecy to last me a lifetime."

Paul held her chin in his hand and tilted her face to his: "No more secrets. I promise you that. Well, actually, there is something."

Ali's heart sank.

"When I was fifteen I borrowed my sister Jan's blue satin blouse and went to a party in it. I thought I looked like a new romantic. It was the eighties, after all."

"Now, if we're talking eighties, I used to wear an old silk nightie that I got in a charity shop with, get this, a turban."

Paul kissed her. "I bet you looked adorable."

Freddie interrupted their kiss by placing his paws on Ali's leg and wagging his tail.

"You know," said Paul. "If Fred could talk, I think he'd have a Liverpudlian accent. He's got that sort of look about him."

Freddie cocked his ears at the sound of his name.

"Oh no, he's definitely from Northern Ireland. I love

that accent, it's so sexy."

Paul looked at her with mock alarm: "My God, you think the dog is sexy! You're seriously weird, you know that. Heaven knows what my mother will make of you."

"Is she still alive? How lucky you are."

"Yes, my Dad too. They'll love you actually."

Paul ran his finger down her nose and onto her lips. "I think I'm falling in love with you myself."

CHAPTER TWENTY-NINE

It no longer surprised Jack how long it would take for Charlie to get ready for an evening out. Being used to Ali, who could shower, change and do her make up in thirty minutes, he had at first been aghast at Charlie's lengthy rituals. Going to the pub would take an hour at least and something special, like tonight's golf dinner, would mean she'd be upstairs for three hours or more.

He knew better than to complain. A mild enquiry as to when she might be ready brought tears and accusations that he didn't want her to look nice. After they'd been late for several occasions, Jack tended to adjust their departure time, telling Charlie they had to leave an hour before they actually did. He could then sit and wait calmly instead of pacing the floor with increasing anxiety.

It was always worth it. When she came downstairs, smiling ruefully because she knew she was late, her beauty took his breath away. For tonight's dinner Charlie was wearing a dress he hadn't seen before, low cut and made of a shimmering golden material. With her blonde curls she looked like a Grecian goddess. She gave a little twirl in front of him, "How do I look?"

"Amazing, ravishing. I'll be the envy of every man there tonight."

He bent down to kiss her lips before changing his mind and pecking her bare shoulder instead. Lipstick renewal could be a lengthy process.

At first, everything went well. There was a tense moment when the club president's wife enquired after Ali but Charlie was busy enchanting the woman's husband and didn't appear to hear. They danced to the band and, when Charlie went to the ladies, Jack, knowing she'd be some time, wandered over to talk to some people at the other side of the room. As he was walking back, a hand gripped his arm.

"Hello, Jack. It's been a while."

Looking down, he saw that it was Sarah Hill. She patted the empty chair next to her and leant towards him. Jack realised that she was rather drunk.

"I see that you've got yourself a new woman. A little young for you, isn't she?"

Jack smiled and gave a shrug. Sarah put her hand on his knee and gazed into his eyes: "Do you miss me, Jack? I think of us often. We were good together, you and me."

She came even closer and he could smell the whiskey on her breath. Before he could move away she kissed him on his mouth.

"What the fuck do you think you are doing! Get your hands off my boyfriend, you old cow."

Jack jumped up off his chair as Charlie pushed Sarah roughly on the shoulder. She leant over her and pointed her finger into Sarah's face: "Get your own man, you bitch!"

Jack tried to take Charlie's hand and lead her away but she shook him off. "Don't touch me! How dare you treat me like this. I turn my back for a minute and come back to find you snogging another woman. And an old wrinkly one at that."

"Oh, I say, that's a bit much."

Sarah's husband Chris had returned to hear Charlie's last remark. He turned to his wife, "What on earth is going on, darling?"

In the presence of another man, Charlie controlled her temper a little and Jack was able to persuade her to leave. As they left the room, Jack caught a glimpse of Carolyn Markham. From her delighted expression he realised that she'd witnessed the whole scene and he saw that she was already turning gleefully to the woman next to her, ready to discuss it in minute detail.

As soon as they got in the car Charlie attacked him. She clawed at his face with her nails and tore his shirt. Even when Jack managed to grab hold of her wrists she continued to scream at him. He saw that it was useless trying to explain until she had calmed down and, eventually, her shouting turned to tears and she let him hold her. He stroked her hair and told that he was sorry that he'd upset her. As she was shivering, he took off his jacket and wrapped it around her before driving home in his ripped shirtsleeves.

He feared another scene when they got back to the house but she went up to bed and fell asleep quite quickly. Jack went downstairs and poured himself a drink. He'd come to know that Charlie was volatile but she'd never been violent towards him before. She was such a passionate woman; that was one of the things he loved about her but he started to wonder if she was a little unstable. Surely her behaviour at the dinner wasn't normal. Perhaps he should end their relationship before he became too involved. He wished that he had someone to discuss it all with. After a while he realised that the person he most wanted to talk to was Ali.

The next morning Jack was relieved to find that Charlie was full of remorse. He'd decided the night before that he'd wait and see what her reaction to her behaviour was. If she was unapologetic and didn't think she'd done anything wrong, then he'd end the relationship. At least, he'd thought he would. Whether he would actually have been able to go through with that was another matter. He wasn't sure that he could be without her now.

Jack had asked Lucy to come over that day and meet Charlie for the first time. Examining the scratches on his cheeks in the bathroom mirror, he thought it would be better to cancel Lucy's visit. How would he explain his ravaged face? However, Lucy's phone seemed to be turned off and, as she was probably already on her way, he'd just have to think of some excuse.

"Dad, wow, that looks nasty. How did you do that?"

"Oh, in the garden. I was cutting down some thorny bushes. It's nothing. It's great to see you. You look lovely."

Jack gave his daughter a hug. She did look well; glowing somehow.

"Come and meet Charlie."

Jack knew that Charlie had been nervous about meeting Lucy and he smiled when he saw how much thought she'd put into her appearance. Her make-up was light and she wore jeans and, unusually for her, a chunky jumper. She came forward and handed Lucy a small carrier bag.

"It's lovely to meet you at last. I've heard so much about you. Here, this is for you."

"Oh, Clinique! I love their products but can never afford them. Thank you so much, Charlie."

"Now, I know that the two of you will have a lot to talk about so I'm going to cook us lunch whilst you just sit in here."

Jack cleared his throat nervously, "Err, are you sure, Charlie? I thought I'd take us to The Feathers."

Jack knew that when she was alone Charlie either ate out or had a salad. Her one attempt at cooking a meal for them both had ended in disaster.

"Yes, absolutely. I've been watching Nigella all week. Just come and open the wine and then leave me to it."

Jack sat with Lucy in the sitting room and, every now and then, put his head around the kitchen door to see how Charlie was doing. Each time she shooed him away, her eyes very bright and he tried not to show his alarm at the increasing disarray in the room. After about thirty minutes, Charlie came into the sitting room proudly holding aloft a large platter.

"An aperitif for you both. Cheese Dreams – enjoy! Lunch won't be much longer."

Jack and Lucy gazed at the blackened triangles. From each one, orange cheese oozed unappetisingly. They tried to not to look at one another. Jack picked up one and took a tentative bite.

"I don't know about Cheese Dreams; these are more like Cheese Nightmares."

Both he and Lucy collapsed into silent laughter.

A short while later, Charlie called to Jack from the kitchen: Darling, do you think you could run out and get some eggs?"

"No need, I bought a dozen yesterday. They should be in the…"

Jack's words faltered as he walked into the room. There were egg shells on every surface and Charlie was clutching a glass of wine and swaying slightly. She started to giggle, "The recipe says to use one egg yolk but the rest of the egg keeps slipping in, look."

She held up a large bowl containing several broken eggs. "I've used them all up now."

Jack scooped up one yolk and put it into another bowl.

"Oh you're so clever. You're a clever, clever man."

Charlie came over to him and wrapped her arms around his waist. Looking down, Jack could see what appeared to be half a bread stick caught in one of her curls. He bent over to kiss her.

"Is everything OK in here?" Lucy looked into the room and Jack and Charlie pulled apart hastily.

"Absolutely. No problemo. Five minutes, six maximum. Go away both of you, shoo."

The lunch, when it finally came, was inedible. The fish was burnt, the potatoes were hard and the dill sauce had an odd taste which Jack couldn't quite identify, but thought may have been marmite. They all pushed the food around their plates and Jack worried that Charlie would be upset but, not long after they'd sat down, she said that she was tired so she was going to have a lie down.

When he drove Lucy back to the station, Jack turned to his daughter and said, "I'm sorry, darling. That didn't go quite as well as I'd hoped."

"It was fine, honestly, Dad. And I really liked Charlie for making all that effort for me; even if it was terrible." She looked at her father solemnly: "Do you mind if I ask you something though, Dad?"

"No, of course not. What is it?"

"Do you think we could stop at McDonald's on the way. I'm absolutely starving."

CHAPTER THIRTY

As Jack had done, the first thing that Ali noticed about her daughter was how wonderful she looked; she glowed with happiness. Ali had received a small but unexpected pre-Christmas bonus from Cassell Brookes and Little and she'd decided to fly back and spend a few days with Lucy. She'd booked them into a smart hotel near Bath and she was looking forward to visiting galleries and spending some time with her daughter.

As she waited in the hotel's elegant lounge, Ali felt that things seemed to be finally going right for her. She and Paul had become increasingly close and it was a long time since she'd woken up each morning full of anticipation about the day ahead. Paul was such an easy man to be with; invariably positive and good humoured. Although she was longing to see Lucy, she knew that she'd be very happy to return to Compesita and Paul's arms. She hadn't told him that she loved him, not yet, but she smiled as she imagined saying those words to him and him saying them back.

Her smile became even broader when Lucy walked in looking so lovely.

"Mum! You're looking very pleased with yourself. Have you hit the Champers already?"

After they'd checked into their room and unpacked, Ali suggested that they have a quick lunch in the hotel bar before going to an exhibition which Ali particularly wanted to see. Over soup and toasted sandwiches, Ali discovered the reason for Lucy's radiance; Tom. Ali had noticed that his name was being mentioned with great regularity but she hadn't realised until now how deep her daughter's feelings for this man were. She couldn't stop talking about him.

"He's so kind, Mum. He helps out at the refuge and all the women love him. And he's clever too. I didn't know it at first but he read law at Cambridge. I think his parents –

On Mum, you should see their house, you'd love it, it's amazing – anyway, I think they're a bit disappointed that he's working on a building site instead at some smart law firm. Honestly, you think they'd just be proud of him, don't you think?"

Ali gave a non-committal murmur. Lucy took a bite of her sandwich and continued: "He's really tall, Mum, taller than Dad and he's very good looking. Well, I think so. Here, look, here's a picture of us outside his house."

Lucy held her phone up and beamed at her mother.

"Anyway, Mum, how about you? Are you still seeing Paul? I think Tom's a nice name, don't you? His mother's a barrister. I told her that you were a solicitor. Oh, and Tom's uncle is quite a well-known artist; isn't that exciting?"

By the end of the day Ali felt that she knew as much about Tom as his own mother did, probably a bit more. But she was thrilled to see her daughter so happy. And Tom did seem to be a good man although she wasn't sure what would happen if he did go and work with disadvantaged people abroad. She couldn't see Lucy coping without TV or her hair straighteners.

On their second day they went for a long walk by the river and Lucy told Ali about the disastrous lunch that Charlie had cooked.

"She seemed nice though, Mum. A bit hyper maybe. I think Dad's quite keen on her. Do you mind? You're happy now aren't you, Mum?"

Ali put her arm through her daughter's arm. "Do you know, I am. I really like Paul. I can't wait for you to meet him. I think you'd like him too."

Every evening before dinner, Ali had taken her notebook into the hotel bar to Skype Paul, leaving Lucy in their room to have another of her endless calls to Tom. Ali told Paul about their day: "I bought a dress this morning on the way to the gallery. I thought that it was really classy and then, as she handed me the bag, the sales assistant announced proudly that the same dress had been worn last week on TV by that really tarty barmaid in that soap – you know, the one that you pretend you never watch?"

Paul laughed: "The girl with the amazing boobs? I can't wait to see you in that. You drive the old boys in the village crazy."

Just before they said goodbye, Paul said that he'd got some exciting news for her: "I won't tell you what it is yet but I think you'll be pleased. I am."

On the plane back to Spain, Ali wondered what Paul's news could be. He'd finished the book he was writing so it was probably something to do with that. He hoped that he would tell her that his publisher loved it and wanted to commission another.

As Ali wouldn't get back to Casa Lucia until late in the evening, she'd arranged to meet Paul for lunch the following day. When she woke up in the morning she felt that she couldn't wait to see him and, although it was still early, she decided to drive round to see him straight away.

The shutters were still closed when she arrived but, as he never locked the door, Ali pushed it open and walked into the hall. She felt a tremor of excitement at the thought of surprising Paul in bed. The stairs to the first floor lay to the right of her and, walking up the stairs with her back to Ali, was a young woman. She was wearing only a man's shirt which barely covered her slender legs and she had long, honey blonde hair which tumbled over her shoulders. Ali was about to speak when the woman said, "Paul, wake up you lazy thing. I've made us some breakfast."

Ali stepped backwards out of the hallway and gently pulled the door to. Her heart was racing and she stood for a minute staring at the ground before getting into her car and driving away. She drove in a daze back to Casa Lucia and stumbled inside. She poured herself a glass of water and tried to think clearly about what she had just seen.

A young woman was staying with Paul. A young woman had made him – them – breakfast in bed. A young woman who was wearing nothing but a man's shirt; she recognised it as one of Paul's.

No matter how many times Ali ran through the scene in her head she couldn't avoid the conclusion that Paul, not expecting to see her until lunchtime, had slept with another woman last night; and, for all she knew, every night that she'd been away. An old familiar misery swept over her. Her heart, so recently healed, felt torn apart once again. What a fool she'd been to think that she'd found happiness.

She was enormously tired and lay on her bed, under the covers. Her phone rang several times but she didn't move. At some point, she heard Paul outside, calling her name and knocking on the door but, after a while, he went away and she was alone again.

At three in the morning, her phone rang again and she picked it up without thinking, "Ali, it's Carl. The baby's coming. Can you get on a plane and come over straight away? Linda's asking for you."

CHAPTER THIRTY-ONE

Sarah Hill was on her fourth cleaner, having finally decided to sack Mrs Keeling when she made a reference to Sarah's drinking, asking if it "wasn't a little early to be starting on the gin"? The first three were hopeless; one talked too much (and usually sat down to do so), another failed to return after the first week and the third brought her small son with her. It wasn't the child that Sarah objected to so much as the fact that she'd returned unexpectedly one afternoon to find little Wayne hoovering the carpet while his mother sat on the sofa flicking through Sarah's Good Housekeeping magazine.

The latest one, Jill, was a short plump woman in her early thirties who raced through her chores and dealt with Sarah's demands with cheerful efficiency. Even Chris, who never interfered in household matters, commented that everywhere was looking remarkably spick and span and Sarah began to congratulate herself on finding a treasure.

After the first few weeks Sarah felt confident enough to go out and leave Jill alone. Once or twice she'd returned earlier than she'd indicated but had never found anything amiss; Jill was always busily working in some part of the house.

One day Chris came home at noon, saying that he'd forgotten some papers he needed for a meeting and that he may as well have some lunch, now he was here.

"I hope you're not expecting me to make you anything. I'm meeting Audrey and the girls in town and I'm already late."

"No, no," Chris began to poke around ineffectually in the cupboards. "I expect I'll find something, dear."

"Shall I do some lunch for you?" Jill's face appeared in the kitchen doorway. "It will be no trouble."

Sarah looked doubtful: "Well, just as long as you finish the bathrooms before you go. He's perfectly capable of making himself a sandwich."

Jill opened the fridge. "How about bacon and eggs?"

She held a packet of bacon in front of her large rounded breasts and smiled encouragingly at Chris. He turned reluctantly from this marvellous vision to kiss his wife goodbye. Sarah squirmed away from him, "Mind, silly. You're smudging my lipstick. Make sure you use the extractor fan, Jill. I don't want the whole house to smell of bacon. OK, see you later."

A few days after this Chris came home at lunchtime again, this time giving the excuse that he'd left his phone behind. Sarah had been out when he arrived and she returned to find him sitting in front of a large plate of sausages and mashed potatoes, whilst gazing fondly at the sight of Jill's plump bottom, which was bent over the dishwasher.

Sarah was having lunch with her friend Audrey and some other women from the gym and she had told them about Chris's lunches. They were all of the opinion that, no matter how good a cleaner Jill was, she'd have to go. There was no point in exposing Chris to too much temptation.

"You want to watch that, you know. My Stephen will do practically anything for fried food."

"But she's really overweight; a size 14 at least. I mean, I suppose she's quite pretty in a rather common way but, my God, the size of her arse!"

Audrey sighed: "Men like that sort of thing, Sarah. We starve ourselves to death; I haven't eaten pastry since 1985 but Stephen's idea of a perfect woman is Pamela Anderson, I ask you!"

The other women joined in eagerly, "Martin simply adores Dawn French." And, "Yes, my husband does too."

The waiter came with the dessert menu but they waved him away, enjoying the sight of his taut bottom as he walked back to the kitchen. Discarding his French accent, he hailed the chef in pure Brummie, "Five sticky toffee puddings for table twelve."

The chef looked up in amazement: "The posh skinny women. You're kidding me, right?"

"Yeah, of course I am. Pudding's probably a swear word to them." He put his hand on his hip. "Oh pudding, I've broken a nail."

The chef grinned: "Pudding off, you, and get back to work."

Emma was fed up. It was Friday evening and, as her work colleagues left excitedly discussing their plans for the weekend, all she had to look forward to was two days alone in her cottage with her cats. Earlier that afternoon she'd gone to look for Martin, the man in accounts who'd asked her out for dinner a while ago, thinking that a date with him would be better than nothing. However, his assistant had told her that he'd already left as he was flying to Barcelona for the weekend. She added that she thought he'd gone to watch a football match but that didn't make Emma feel any better.

She looked out of the window. Everywhere people were hailing taxis or walking purposefully towards their destinations. It seemed that everyone in London had somewhere to go except her. Reaching into her desk for her security pass, she noticed her passport. She kept it at work in case, as sometimes happened, she had to travel somewhere unexpectedly. She considered briefly catching a plane to Barcelona and surprising Martin but quickly dismissed the idea. She'd never find him in the crowd and, anyway, a vision of his round bland face reminded her of why she'd refused to have dinner with him in the first place.

On impulse, she turned on her PC again and bought a return Eurostar ticket to Paris. A couple of days wandering around her favourite city was just what she needed to cheer herself up. She could buy a few essentials at St Pancras and treat herself to some new clothes when she got to France. Having reserved a room in a boutique hotel on the left bank, Emma set off for the station, happily merging into the throng of Londoners, all with a Friday night destination in mind.

The train at been at a standstill for over an hour and no one seemed able to give Emma any explanation for the delay. She sighed and put down her magazine. The weekend had been an utter disappointment. Paris had been wet and grey. She'd been unable to find anything she liked in the shops and, needing a change of clothes, had bought a horrendously expensive dress which didn't suit her and which she was now regretting. Even her hotel, a haven of quiet French elegance when she'd stayed there last, was occupied with a large group of women on a hen weekend, who wore T-shirts printed with slogans of staggering crudity and whose screeching disrupted the solitude of the small marble clad bar.

The passengers in Emma's carriage exchanged relieved glances as the train started to move, although one man was heard saying into his phone, "No, dear, still not moving. I don't expect I'll be home tonight."

Opposite Emma was a well-dressed man in his late fifties. He'd been preoccupied with his laptop for much of the journey but, feeling the motion of the train, he looked up and smiled at her. She'd already noticed his expensive clothes and thick, grey hair, which was brushed back from his forehead and now she saw that he had very dark eyes under black arched brows and a square determined chin. His voice, when he spoke, was English; deep, with a faint Northern bur.

"That's a relief. I was beginning to fear we'd be stuck here all night. Do you have far to go when we reach St Pancras?"

Emma told him that she lived in West London and, in answer to his enquiry about her weekend, told him about her disastrous trip. Enjoying how he laughed at her description of the hen party, Emma went on to tell him of her shopping trip, exaggerating both the awfulness of her new outfit and the haughtiness of the Parisian sales assistant, hoping for a repeat of his rich baritone laughter.

They chatted for the rest of the journey and Emma was surprised to find that they were pulling into St Pancras. The man, who'd introduced himself as Michael Easton, had told her that he was the operations director of a major food company. He'd amused her with an account of his trip, which hadn't gone much better than her own. The newly installed manager of his company's Paris office had decided to close down the workplace restaurant and install vending machines in its place. Michael had had to intervene to prevent a mass walk out.

"He's not a Frenchman, you see and hadn't realised that a muesli bar doesn't constitute a proper lunch."

As Michael reached up to the overhead locker for Emma's bag, she noticed his square shoulders and upright frame, aided, no doubt, by the extremely well cut suit he was wearing. As she said goodbye, Emma felt a pang of disappointment that the journey was over.

"It's too late to travel up to Yorkshire tonight. I think I'll stay in town. I don't suppose I can persuade you to join me for a drink? I usually stay at The Savoy. The cocktails in the American bar are really good." Michael looked expectantly at Emma, "Unless there is someone waiting for you at home, that is?"

"No, just the cats. They always sulk when I go away, so they won't be much company anyway."

Damn it, thought Emma, *stop talking about the cats. Now he'll think I'm some mad spinster living alone with twelve Persians.*

"How about you, Michael? Won't your wife mind if you don't get home tonight?"

"It's just me and the dog. He'll probably moan a bit but my sister will keep him for another night."

As the taxi sped towards The Savoy, Emma and Michael each felt a bubble of excitement at the thought of an evening in one another's company. A few cocktails, dinner maybe and then; well, who knows? Emma had been disappointed that her rash decision to go to Paris for the weekend had turned out so badly. Normally, when she acted on impulse, things went well for her. Now it seemed that may be the case.

She turned towards Michael and fleetingly touched his strong square hand. "Do you make a habit of picking up strange women on trains?"

"Only those who wear hideous expensive dresses." He broke into his deep laugh. "Actually, Emma, meeting you has been the nicest thing that has happened to me in ages."

He leant towards her and his lips briefly brushed hers before the taxi pulled up abruptly in front of the hotel. As they were ushered inside, Emma realised that Michael was the first man she'd been attracted to who wasn't Simon.

"Mr Easton. Welcome back, sir. Are you staying with us tonight? I'll just check if your usual room is available."

Emma tried and failed to imagine Simon receiving such a welcome.

After two cocktails in the American bar, Emma felt herself relax properly for the first time in months. She'd intended to go back to her cottage after a quick drink as she had to work in the morning but she found herself agreeing to Michael's suggestion that they go through and have dinner. Over their meal they found that they had many things in common. Like her, Michael was active and adventurous and they discovered that they'd been to many of the same places and had done the same things.

"My true passion is sailing. Have you tried that, Emma? I keep a small yacht near my place down in Poole and I go there as often as I can."

On hearing that sailing was the one thing that Emma had never tried, Michael wanted them both to go the next day.

"The world of finance won't collapse if you play hooky for once, Emma. I have a friend who could fly us down there in the morning."

Both fell silent whilst the implication that they would

spend the night together hung in the air, before Michael changed the subject and asked her what plays she'd seen recently.

Michael name dropped shamelessly; he seemed to know everyone but Emma found that she didn't mind. Maybe it was his age, but Michael had an assurance about him that she liked. His opinion was that you should always try to get the very best out of life and Emma liked that. It helped, of course, if you had the money to do so and Michael appeared to have plenty of that. In addition to his yacht and apartment in Poole, he had mentioned a place in France that he used when he went skiing.

Excusing herself, Emma went to the ladies and sat looking at her reflection in the mirror. She was undecided whether to leave now or to stay and spend the night with Michael. She felt attracted to him but he was much older than any of the other men she'd slept with. Although he looked younger, he'd told her that he was sixty-two; almost the same age as her father. Well, there was only one way to find out if they were sexually compatible and, when she walked back into the bar, instead of sitting down again she held out her hand and said, "Shall we?"

At first Emma thought that she'd made an awful mistake. Naked, Michael's legs looked rather thin and he had a bit of a paunch, which his expensive suit had hidden. His chest was covered in thick, grey hair and he looked a little like a teddy bear, she thought, supressing a giggle. The other thing was, although he had quite an impressive erection, it wasn't pressed straight up against his stomach, as she was used to, but sort of bobbled out at a right angle.

When he started to caress her, however, she soon realised what a skilful lover he was. He was so attentive, so giving, that her body quickly responded. He made her feel beautiful; not just with his words but by his actions too. She felt as though she was the most desirable woman in the world. Lying in his arms afterwards, Emma thought how selfish her other, younger, lovers had been in bed; it was always about pleasing them. With Michael, she felt cossetted and, drifting off to sleep, Emma realised that she liked the feeling.

They'd agreed the previous night to postpone their sailing trip to the following weekend and Emma had set her phone to wake her at six, so that she could go home to change before heading into the office. When her alarm went off, she was surprised to find that Michael was already up. She could hear him in the adjoining bathroom and so she lay back for a few more minutes, enjoying the large bed and the beautiful 1930s furnishings in the room. Michael's phone rang and she lazily reached across to look at the screen, so that she could tell him of his missed call.

"Well good morning. You look even more beautiful than you did last night."

Michael sat on the bed in his bathrobe and kissed her. Emma raised her eyebrows. She knew how she normally looked in the mornings and it certainly wasn't beautiful. However, glancing in the mirror opposite the bed, she saw that she did have a sort of sultry sexiness about her. With her blonde hair tousled against the crumpled sheets, she looked like an actress in a French film. Enjoying the moment, she tossed her hair and pouted a little. Michael, too, was perfectly cast as the older lover.

"Your phone's just rung. It was Stella. Is that your sister?."

"Yes." Michael sat down on the bed. "Actually, no. I should tell you, Emma. I want to tell you. Stella is my wife."

On the taxi journey back to her cottage, Emma thought about Michael's words. After the revelation that he was married, she had wanted to walk out immediately but he'd pleaded with her to allow him to explain. He'd told her that his wife, Stella, had been ill for many years. Before they'd become aware of her condition, they had been about to separate. Stella had been having an affair and she wanted to leave.

"When she told me that she was ill and that her condition was only going to get worse, I couldn't abandon her. The chap she'd been seeing disappeared and she was so frightened and alone. So, I stayed. We have separate rooms and I'm away a lot, so we manage somehow. A woman from the village comes every day and my sister is very good."

Emma had conflicting emotions. She could see that Michael was a good man for not walking away from his sick wife but she was angry with him for not telling her about his situation before she spent the night with him. He'd agreed wholeheartedly with her on that: "I should have told you, I know that but I wanted you so much. And I don't have a wife, not in any true sense of the word. I will understand, though, if you feel that you don't want to see me again. Can I just ask you not to decide now but to think about it for a few days? I'll telephone you on Wednesday at twelve o'clock. If you don't pick up then I'll know what your answer is."

Emma tried not to think about Michael all day at work but her mind kept returning to funny things he'd said or places that he wanted to take her to. Halfway through the morning an enormous bouquet of flowers was delivered to her office with a note that said: "Forgive me. Michael".

After lunch, a courier arrived with an envelope containing two tickets for a concert she'd mentioned that she wanted to go to. On the back Michael had written: "Take a friend and enjoy". The gifts only compounded a vague but growing feeling of shame Emma was becoming aware of about her night with Michael. Now that the thrill at her audacity had worn off, she felt a little ashamed of her actions. Would she have slept with him if he hadn't been so obviously rich?

Finding it impossible to concentrate on her work, Emma left the office early and returned to the cottage. She busied herself in finding vases for the flowers before sitting on the sofa with a drink. She knew that with Michael she'd enjoy her life; he'd spoil her and take her to new and exciting places. She'd always wanted to learn how to sail and it would be wonderful to be able to fly to his chalet and ski whenever she wanted. And it wasn't as though he and his wife were really together. They'd have been divorced long ago if she hadn't fallen ill and the fact that he'd stayed with her showed his caring nature.

Emma knew that the story about Michael's wife was true. He'd mentioned that he knew her boss slightly and so, in the office, she'd introduced Michael into the conversation and had asked her boss casually if he'd ever met Stella.

"Michael Easton's wife? No, never. I don't think she ever comes to London. In fact, I have a feeling that she's an invalid of some kind, poor woman."

Emma winced at her boss's description. It was typical of him to use such an offensive word but she was pleased that Michael had been telling the truth.

On Wednesday morning at noon Emma's phone rang. Seeing Michael's name on the screen, she left the phone on her desk and walked out of the office. After all those years yearning for Simon, she'd promised herself that she'd find someone who would put her first; someone for whom she was the only woman in their life. And, unfortunately, that wasn't Michael.

CHAPTER THIRTY-TWO

ONE YEAR LATER

Ali drove to the airport to pick up Linda, Carl and baby Laura. She hadn't seen Laura for six months and, although they Skyped often and the sight of Laura's red curls was the highlight of Ali's week, she couldn't wait to pick her up and squeeze her. She got there far too early and Ali knew that the people streaming through the arrivals gate had been on the Manchester flight and she had another forty minutes before the Gatwick plane landed.

Suddenly, something caught her eye and she stopped to get a better look. There was no mistaking those long, coltish legs and cascading blonde hair. Ali glanced to her right and, as she expected, walking behind the young woman was Paul. He was pulling a bright pink suitcase and wearing a black T-shirt which was far too young for him. Even so, the sight of him made Ali's heart lurch and she stepped behind a pillar so that she could watch them both surreptitiously. A large man greeting his even larger wife blocked Ali's view for a moment and, when the pair had finally waddled away, Paul was nowhere to be seen. Ali scanned the crowd and was about to walk away when a hand grabbed her wrist, "Aren't you going to say hello?"

Paul stood before her. She could see that the woman he was with was having a cigarette outside. Ali took a step backwards and looked him up and down. "I almost didn't recognise you in that ridiculous T-shirt."

All at once they flung their arms around each other and hugged tightly. Paul swung her into the air, "My God, have you put on weight?"

They smiled into each other's faces delightedly. "Ella's gone to have a fag. She forced me to spend a fortune in Duty Free. It's a good job I've only got one daughter."

When Paul and Ella had driven away, Ali went to get a coffee and thought back to the dreadful time a year ago when she'd assumed that Ella was Paul's lover. It had never even crossed her mind that she could be his daughter; they hadn't seen one another for so many years. In her mind, Ella was a schoolgirl, not the self-assured beauty she'd become.

After Linda's baby had been born, Ali, having no desire to return to Compesita, stayed on with her and Carl, helping them to cope with new parenthood. Not that they'd need much help; both were in their element. Carl, in particular, was wonderful with Laura, carrying her round all day against his naked chest. He'd read somewhere that it helped with bonding but it always made Linda giggle and she said that she hoped to God that he'd stop it before Laura went to school.

One afternoon, when Ali had been there for a couple of weeks, she was alone in the house when there was a knock on the door. Going into the hall, she could see Paul through the glass panel and she shouted at him to go away. Since she'd arrived, he'd called and texted her several times a day but she'd ignored all of his messages; she had no wish to speak to him, or any man, for as long as she lived. She'd half expected him to turn up at the house and she was determined to let him know that he'd had a wasted journey.

"Ali, please. I don't know why you are doing this. Why did you run away? Was it something I did?"

"Ha, you could say that; or *someone* you did, anyway."

"I have absolutely no idea what you're talking about. Please, just let me in and we can clear this up."

"Never. I don't want to speak to you or see your face ever again. Can't you understand that? I hate you."

"Whatever it is that you think I have done, you're mistaken. I love you. I'm dying without you. Ali, please."

The desolation in Paul's voice touched Ali but she steeled herself against his words; they were nothing but lies.

"Look, if you don't want to be with me anymore then OK but at least you could tell me why. I deserve that surely?"

"Deserve? That's rich. I deserved a man who was faithful but you couldn't do that, could you. Paul?"

"Faithful? Ali, I've always been faithful to you. There has never been anyone else for me since the day I first saw you at that bar."

"Huh, what about blondie? At Jan's house, bringing you a cosy breakfast in bed? I called round to see you. I couldn't wait, stupid fool that I am but I saw her instead, wearing your shirt."

Paul started to laugh and it incensed Ali even more.

"I'm glad that you think it's funny, Paul. Let me tell you, you broke my heart. I loved you and you just threw it back in my face."

"Ali, Ali darling, that was Ella, my daughter. It was my surprise for you. Do you remember? She got in touch out of the blue and came out to see me. She's my daughter, Ali."

Ali had been hurting for so many weeks that her initial reaction was to disbelieve him. However, after a few moments she realised that this wasn't something that he could make up; it would be too easy to disprove. Small tentacles of hope began to weave their way into her mind.

"Ali, did you hear me? Are you still there? You do believe me, don't you? I can get her on the phone if you like."

"Yes, I believe you."

"Thank God. In that case, do you think I could come inside? It's absolutely freezing out here."

They made up in the best way possible in Linda's spare bed. When Linda and Carl returned home they were amazed to find Ali dancing around the kitchen making cheese on toast for her and Paul. Linda was sceptical at first but, when Paul told them about his daughter getting in touch, of how they'd talked on the phone for hours and how he'd impulsively booked her a flight to Spain the next day, she accepted that it was all true.

"Do you mean that we've had all this moping about for no reason? She was supposed to be looking after me but she's been that miserable."

Linda looked at her sister fondly: "You are a daft cow."

Lying in Paul's arms that night Ali stroked his chest and said, "How did you know where to find me?"

"Oh, I called everyone I could think of. Lucy told me you were here and gave me the address. She didn't want to at first but I said that I was in love with you and how would she feel if Tom just suddenly disappeared from her life without a word? I said that she would have to know what had happened and she gave in and told me."

"There aren't any other surprises are there? You're not the love child of Margaret Thatcher or a Russian spy or something?"

He kissed her hair. "No, well only that you might want to think about marrying me sometime. I know that it wouldn't be much fun for you but just think of how nice it would be for me."

Ali stood at the kitchen window and watched the small group on the terrace. Lucy and Tom had arrived that morning and Paul's daughter Ella the day before and so, with Linda, Carl and Laura, the house was full and it was wonderful. Her friend, Emma, was supposed to be there too but she'd called Ali the week before to say that would she mind if she put her trip off for a month or two as she'd been invited to go to North Wales.

"North Wales? Didn't you go there a few weeks ago? To do that abseiling thing? I thought you said that it was cold, everyone was about twelve and that you hated it?"

"Well only the first few days. It sort of got better after that."

"Sort of warmer better or good looking instructor better?"

"Instructor better. God, Als, you should see him. Black curly hair, blue eyes and the most amazing biceps. I'd got myself tangled up in the harness thing and he just lifted me up with one finger practically. Then I found that I'd hurt my leg a bit and so he carried me all the way back to the hostel. Ran most of the way. Amazing."

"OK, well you have fun is it, with this boyo."

There was a short silence on the line.

"Was that supposed to be a Welsh accent?"

Ali laughed: "Yes, sorry. It came out a bit West Country. Anyway, have a good time. We'll all miss you. What happened with the rich old guy; the one in the Savoy?"

"Well, he called loads of times and sent masses of flowers but I didn't reply and eventually he gave up. He even sent this fabulous hamper from Fortnum and Mason with a note saying let's go for a picnic. I sent it back. I kept the Champagne, obvs."

Ali and Paul had bought the old cortijo nine months ago. They'd found it during one of their walks in the hills above Compesita; a long, low farmhouse in a poor state of repair but with fabulous views and its own almond and olive groves. From the money Ali had received from the sale of her house in Westwood and some savings of Paul's, they had been able to afford to pay a builder to carry out all of the major work required. They'd stayed in Casa Lucia until most of the repairs were done but the little house was much too small for two, even when the pair were very much in love.

The decorating they'd done themselves and Ali had gone for a Moorish feel, painting the internal walls in deep oranges and reds and scattering the low cream sofas they'd bought with jewel coloured cushions. She and Paul worked together well; Ali did most of the inside jobs whilst Paul worked hard in the garden. Ali looked everywhere for old pieces of furniture which she'd take up onto the roof terrace to rub down and restore.

One day when Ali was up on the roof as usual finishing off a large pine chest, she called to Paul on the terrace below: "Hey, Paul, could you come up here and take my drawers down?"

He grinned up at her: "I thought you said you were busy."

Ali had taken the job with her old client John Drake and, as she could work from anywhere as long as it had internet connection, they divided their time between the cortijo and Paul's Manchester apartment. Paul's book had been well received and he was often invited to give lectures at other universities, sometimes abroad. He'd arranged to limit his teaching at his own university to one term a year, to allow him the freedom to travel and to write another book. They were very happy together; content with one another's company for weeks at a time but always pleased to have other people around them too.

The family group all got on well together. Everyone doted on baby Laura; the minute she woke up, she was carried round and played with. There was always someone waiting to cuddle the plump little package.

"I don't know how we'll cope when it's just the two of us again," said Linda, sinking back into the sofa whilst Lucy and Ella swooped on a delighted Laura and ran with her into the garden.

Later on, when she and Ali were in the kitchen making dinner, Linda brought the subject up again.

"Actually, Als, we've been thinking of asking Carl's Mum to live with us. Now that I'm back at work it would be much easier to have her on hand to look after Laura."

"Well, that's a big step, Lin. Are you still getting on well with her?"

"Really well. I mean, she still gets on my nerves sometimes. The other weekend, when she was down, I asked her if she wanted any breakfast and she said, 'Oh, I never have breakfast, dear; a yoghurt, some cereal and a couple of pieces of toast sees me through until at least eleven o'clock.'"

The sisters laughed and Linda continued: "And Grandma lived with us when we were little and we loved it, didn't we?"

"Yes, but Grandma was so kind and easy to be with. Remember how nice she was when you got suspended from school that time and Mum and Dad freaked out?"

"God, yes, she was amazing. She said that she'd left school at fourteen and it hadn't done her any harm."

The sisters peeled vegetables in silence for a while before Linda asked, "How is your old friend Carolyn doing? Do you hear from her much these days?"

Ali paused, holding a half peeled potato: "We didn't really speak for a while. I was angry with her for siding with Jack. But I called her a few months ago and now we Skype every week or so. We're getting there. I don't think our friendship will ever be as close as it was but it's not her fault what happened. And she does make me laugh. Remember her husband, Trevor? Well apparently he's grown his sideburns and had his eyes lasered. She says he looks like a '70s geography teacher; she quite likes it, apparently."

Tom was very interested in the old irrigation system that Paul had unearthed in the orchard and he spent long hours helping to clear it of generations of silt and weeds. Lucy carried out mugs of tea for him and would sit, watching him work, stretching out her bare legs to catch the sun. She didn't need to tell Ali of her happiness; it was evident in her shining eyes. Ali didn't know if their relationship would last, they were both still so young, but she liked Tom and thanked God again that her daughter had recovered from the time with Mason. Lucy had spoken of it briefly that afternoon, telling her mother that she'd heard that Mason had been sent to prison. She wasn't quite sure what for but thought it was something to do with changing the mileage on second hand cars. Lucy spoke of it quite matter-of-factly and Ali hoped that the time in prison might make Mason change his ways, but doubted that it would.

Lucy and Ella had bonded straight away. Ali, who had often regretted the fact that Lucy had no siblings, fondly watched as the pair tried on each other's clothes and debated which university Ella should go to; it seemed as though Lucy now had the sister she'd always wanted.

Two sisters, possibly. Lucy had, rather hesitantly, told Ali the night before that Charlie was having Jack's baby. She'd looked carefully at her mother when she'd said this, gaging her reaction closely. Ali had felt a pang of something when she heard; not quite regret and certainly not jealousy but a slight pull towards the past. However, she had smiled at her daughter and told her that she was happy for them both. Later, when Ali was alone, she wondered how Jack would cope with a baby again at his age and smiled a little to herself at the thought of him once again having to get up in the middle of the night and the long games of golf he'd now have to forgo.

Everyone took it in turns to cook or they'd walk into Compesita and eat in one of the bars there. On one such evening, Ali sat at the head of the table, proudly watching the animated group chatting away to one another; Carl pacing up and down with Laura on his hip, Tom earnestly telling Ella about the charity he hoped to work for, Linda and Lucy giggling over the waiter, who'd taken a shine to Linda; and Paul, sitting opposite her and smiling at her with eyes filled with love.

Ali glanced over at the little corner bar at the other side of the square and remembered sitting there the first time she'd come to Compesita. How much her life had changed since then; so much had happened and most of it good, really good. She thought of Sarah Hill, who'd been the reason that Ali had come to Compesita on her own in the first place. Carolyn had told her, during one of their Skype sessions, that it was all over the village that Sarah was having an affair with the pro at the golf club.

"Honestly, darling, how unimaginative. It will be her

tennis coach next. Her swings improved though, I'll give her that much."

On the day everyone was to go home, they sat in the kitchen, having a late breakfast. Lucy helped herself to another piece of toast and said, "Oh, there's a letter for you, Mum, over there on the dresser."

Ali picked up the large brown envelope and took it into the garden. Opening it, she sat quietly for a moment. Her marriage to Jack was officially over. It had been over for ages, of course, but she did feel a sense of pity at reading the words. Not regret, because she was so happy now, happier than perhaps she'd ever been, but the end of a marriage must surely bring with it some shades of sadness.

Paul came out of the house and looked at her with concern.

"I was wondering where you'd got to."

Ali smiled at him. "Yes."

Paul smiled back. "Yes what?"

"Yes, I will marry you. I think I'd like that very much."